DEVILISH GAMES

RED GARNIER

ELLORA'S CAVE
ROMANTICA PUBLISHING

SPIN DEVIL

When her college friends suggest an intimate reunion in Florida, Cleo Sonterra has reservations. She's anxious about seeing Sebastian Russo again, the man who taunted and tormented her for four years. His dark good looks don't disguise the fact that he's the meanest bastard she's ever met. It would be great to see her friends again—if she can just remain completely unaffected by Sebastian.

At the beach, drinks flow and inhibitions are loosened while the friends play an adult version of Truth or Dare, mixed with Spin the Bottle, using a stuffed toy instead. As the plush devil spins and the truths and dares become more risky, Cleo is faced with the single most frightening dare of all. Because Sebastian Russo is the same bad boy he's always been—and thanks to the spin devil, Cleo's about to find out how bad he can be.

SPIN IT AGAIN

It's been a year since the night David Hawthorne played spin devil. During that wild night of drinks and dares, he'd gambled with his future and lost his fiancé. His life has been a living nightmare ever since, a dark and desolate wasteland where no amount of cheap booze and cheaper sex will erase Evie from his mind. David would do anything to win her back, even if it means spinning that hateful toy devil…again.

Evie Mathews never thought David would betray her but oh, how wrong she'd been. She's painfully reminded of him at every turn, when all she wants is to forget him—but David won't let her. He storms back into her life, a crazed, angry shadow of the man she remembers, and demands they play the very game that tore them apart a year ago. But this time, the game has only one possible outcome.

SPIN SOME MORE

Convinced the spin devil was ruining his sex life, Jason gave the stuffed toy to his neighbor, Penelope. Now if only he could get rid of *her* as easily. She's driving him out of his head with lust. Problem is, he's made it his mission to protect her — especially from men like *him*.

Penelope has tried everything to entice Jason with her wiles, resulting in zero progress. He still sees her as the sweet, innocent girl he grew up with. Now she has a little red friend who might help her get what she wants, and if she has her way, the devil won't be the only one spinning tonight.

An Ellora's Cave Romantica Publication

www.ellorascave.com

Devilish Games

ISBN 9781419962196
ALL RIGHTS RESERVED.
Spin Devil Copyright © 2007 Red Garnier
Spin It Again Copyright © 2007 Red Garnier
Spin Some More Copyright © 2007 Red Garnier
Edited by Kelli Collins.
Cover art by Willo.

Trade paperback publication 2010

This book is a work of fiction and any resemblance to persons, living or dead, or places, events or locales is purely coincidental. The characters are productions of the author's imagination and used fictitiously.

DEVILISH GAMES

Red Garnier

ଔ

SPIN DEVIL
~9~

SPIN IT AGAIN
~57~

SPIN SOME MORE
~101~

SPIN DEVIL

Trademarks Acknowledgement

ℬ

The author acknowledges the trademarked status and trademark owners of the following wordmarks mentioned in this work of fiction:

Frisbee: Wham-O, Inc.

Chapter One

ဆာ

It had been four years.

The six friends had parted ways after college with a last night of drinks, dancing and sex. Cleo Sonterra remembered the night full well, for it was the night she and David had made love after months of flirting, taunting and teasing. He'd made love to her in his dorm room, in a small rumpled bed, with the lights turned off. Cleo had expected him to be thorough and tender, but in reality he'd been shaky, clumsy and too drunk to think coherently. Her lack of enthusiasm hadn't helped matters much, and that was only because she'd been thinking of someone else entirely—someone she *shouldn't* have been thinking of at that moment.

It was the first time Cleo and David had sex—and the last.

It had been a night such as this, friends gathered out on the beach with a bonfire that blazed high and mighty toward the dark skies. Tonight there was no massive fire except for the flames blazing in the six pairs of eyes present, and that was merely a reflection of the flickering orange lights from the dozens of steel lanterns scattered over the sand.

They sat in a circle on thick old blankets strewn around the sand, the lulling sound of the ocean's waves crashing against the shore a very distant second to the loud sounds of their laughter. Several yards behind them stood the two-story contemporary beachfront house where Jason now lived. His home encompassed a good stretch of beach on the east coast of Florida.

The six friends were playing an old college game, this time with a plush red devil—complete with pitchfork and tail—that Luella had brought from Los Angeles. It was a

11

strange little toy, covered in smooth, shiny red satin and a bit too heavy for its size, with dark, beady eyes that seemed to stare right through you. Despite the toy's strangely unsettling appearance, all of the friends had been more than willing to give it a spin.

So the devil had replaced the bottle, and the truths and dares had become extreme and, yes, devilishly sinful. This was no longer a game played by college students. It was a game played by consenting adults who were very drunk...and maybe just a little horny.

Personally, Cleo had had her reservations about attending the reunion. First and foremost because she had no desire to see their group "leader", a man with absolutely no affection for her—and one with no scruples, either. Sebastian Russo cheated at cards, lied at his leisure, stole to prove that he could, smoked, drank, cursed and whored to his liking. He had always teased and taunted Cleo mercilessly for being what he considered a "damned prude"—as if he were an authority on the subject, when he had zero principles to speak of. He clearly couldn't comprehend why Cleo preferred to cuddle at home with a book rather than get drunk every single day—like *he* usually did. And although her friends, Luella and Haley, didn't drink that often either, Sebastian would *only* tease Cleo about it.

Yet no matter how much she dreaded facing him, Cleo missed her friends as much as she missed her college years. Every moment they'd shared—the tender, the wild, the sad, the first and the last. Luella and Haley had even threatened to fly up to Seattle and haul her down to Florida if she didn't get her butt down here to their reunion.

"You *have* to come. We all want to see you, we really miss you, sweetie," Luella had said on the phone a few weeks ago. "Even all the guys have been wanting to know if you're coming...well, except Bas, but you know how he is."

Of course Cleo knew how he was, and just knowing he probably didn't *want* her to go, because to him she was just a "damned prude" who would only spoil his fun, Cleo decided she *had* to go. She couldn't—and wouldn't—let the fear of facing one man keep her from enjoying a lovely reunion with the rest of her friends.

When Cleo first arrived at Jason's place, she'd felt awkward and shy, noting how each of her friends had grown during the past years. All of them looked more mature, the years gone by somehow etched in their brows, the spark of experience glimmering in their eyes. But now, hours later, she gazed at each of them while they drank and smoked and dared and laughed, and realized that time had not changed them. They were still the dear, reckless friends she'd known before.

Jason was still as handsome as she remembered, with his tanned jock's body and regal blond hair. He played professional golf now and she'd often seen his familiar face on TV, brow usually furrowed in concentration as he focused on his swing. Jason rarely found fault in anything, and his easygoing, carefree manner accounted for the dozens of times someone had pulled him aside to spill his or her guts to him, treating him like a shrink. Jason didn't mind at all. In fact, he seemed to enjoy having an excuse to laze around quietly and do nothing more than nod.

Being his complete opposite and a man who inspired nothing but shivers, Sebastian Russo was as dark as night, and as reckless and rude as ever. For some cruel reason the years had only enhanced his masculinity, something he seemed blatantly aware of—and which he used to his advantage. His eyes, those coal-black eyes, hawk-like and narrowed under the vicious slashes of his eyebrows, served as weapons to issue unspoken threats and bend his targets to his will—be they man or woman. There was strength in his face, in his brow, in the straightness of his nose and the firmness of jaw, as if he'd been cast in iron—which could account for his seeming inability to smile or grin or laugh.

He wore his thick mass of silken black hair longer now, falling past his ears with a light curl at the ends. His hair and his luscious full lips were his mildest characteristics — though not necessarily the least threatening. The truth was, just by sitting there, Sebastian managed to engulf the space surrounding him like a black hole — consuming and overpowering everything around him. Cleo had no idea what he did for a living but she imagined it was something that fit his vicious black heart. Maybe even killing for hire.

Then there was David — tall, distinguished-looking David, who was a man with ideals, with goals. A man known throughout college for his kindness and sensitivity as well as for his hard work and ambition. No matter how big a salary he was earning on Wall Street, he still looked every bit the studious, clean-cut frat guy Cleo had always known. Of course, he'd grown even more gorgeous during the years, his sculpted face now firmer, stronger, having lost some of the boyish qualities that Cleo had found so attractive when they'd met during their first year at college.

Next was Luella, who'd highlighted her light brown hair with silky blonde streaks. Though she now looked every inch the bombshell with her new boobs, she was still the same foul-mouthed smoker Cleo knew so well. Enjoy life to its fullest was Luella's motto. There was probably nothing she wouldn't try and no feat too impossible for her to tackle. Even if it *was* impossible, she'd never let that keep her from trying. She worked in real estate now and she sometimes slept with her clients to celebrate a purchase, so she thought her job was "fucking great".

Then came the spirited, talkative Haley, a recently confessed fashion freak since she'd lost a few pounds. Now her body, although petite, was curvaceous and enticing, her long, wavy hair blazing red under the glow of the flickering lantern lights. She was a publicist at a tobacco company and had brought free smokes for them all — which had been, for the most part, consumed by Sebastian.

And finally Cleo. Shy, sweet Cleo, who wore the same solid, conservative dresses she used to wear — the ones that hid her uncomfortable C-cup breasts rather well—and her shiny black hair in the usual neat bun at her nape.

Unlike Haley and Luella, Cleo disliked colorful, revealing clothes, and because they were so uncomfortable and impractical, she religiously stayed away from high heels. She preferred flat, pretty sandals. Rather than wear heavy makeup, she used gloss on her lips and a natural blush to add color to her cheeks. Her face was too doll-like to accept much makeup anyway. Her lips were heart shaped, small and pouty, while her eyes were big, dark brown in color, framed by rows of eyelashes Luella and Haley had repeatedly sworn they'd kill for. Her hair was long, though she rarely wore it loose, and it was so dark it made her skin look even fairer, a porcelain white that was unfortunately much too sensitive to see the sun for long.

None of her friends had ever been bothered by her plain appearance except *him*. His face had turned into a dark, unyielding mask of disapproval the moment she stepped on the beach. And if she thought she'd be able to see him again without being the least bit affected, she'd been sorely mistaken.

She'd had two beers up until now, only because the occasion warranted she drink something, while the rest of her friends had had dozens, and it was hard to keep from smiling at their antics and their dares. The retirement home where she worked seemed worlds away from here, her drunken friends proving a stark contrast to the solemn, somber old people she looked after. When they misbehaved, the old people smuggled chocolates into the home and played harmless pranks on some of the nurses, while her friends…were another story.

"Okay, spin it!" Luella called.

Needing no more prodding, Jason took the devil between his thumb and forefinger and with a flick of his wrist sent it spinning over a large Frisbee they'd set on the sand in the center of the circle. It suddenly stopped, the pitchfork pointing

15

straight at Sebastian, the tail at Cleo. Cheers erupted, yet Cleo couldn't help but feel rather nervous.

"Sebastian, it's time to pay the rent, old boy," Luella said with a wicked smile twitching her lips.

"Come on, Cleo, give him a good one," someone encouraged.

Smiling shakily, Cleo looked into Sebastian's deep black eyes. He sat with one leg folded and an arm resting on top of his knee, a cigarette clasped tightly between his thumb and forefinger. His blue jeans were old, faded white over his thighs, and his dark brown leather jacket was slightly torn at the elbows.

Cleo was grateful that she was able to keep her voice steady, since she'd always seemed to have trouble speaking directly to him. "Truth or dare, Sebastian?"

His smile was slow and lazy. "Dare. Of course."

Everyone laughed and Cleo glanced around the circle, her brain racing with thoughts. How did one dare a man who feared nothing? How did one dare a reckless, crazed man who acted like he had a death wish?

The cigarette blazed bright red as Sebastian took a drag, his eyes narrowed above the billow of smoke. It was impossible to dare the devil himself, so she just said the first thing that came to mind. "I dare you to…kiss Luella. On the mouth."

His chest heaved when he grunted. "Is that the worst you can do, Cleo?" He flicked his cigarette into the air. He looked like the devil incarnate, and though they'd all been friends, Cleo had always been secretly afraid of him—because he had the power to hurt her. And he always did.

David laughed beside her. "That really sucked, Cleo."

"Not for *me* it doesn't suck! *Thank you*, sweetie!" Luella said excitedly, sinking the bottom of her beer into the sand before she turned to Sebastian next to her.

Sebastian faced Luella with a wan, lazy smile, so sure of himself and his disgustingly potent sex appeal. He looked casual and confident, as if he did this sort of thing every day, which was probably a correct assumption.

Cleo watched as his big tanned hands cupped Luella's cheeks and he bent forward to kiss her. No matter how many times Cleo had watched Sebastian kiss someone—which at college had been more times than she'd cared to count—it never failed to shock her. His victims always unfailingly reacted the same way—in a way Cleo thought the feminists in the country would greatly disapprove.

It was as if he hypnotized them, and within seconds they would be limp in his arms and breathing fast and furiously. He, on the other hand, would drop his hands as if he'd finished doing something as mundane as brushing his teeth, and look as unmoved as a mountain during a storm.

Cleo had thought about this repeatedly during the years. Although Sebastian's eyes were enough to send a woman running for cover, she wondered what it was about his mouth and those strong, powerful lips that could melt almost anything they touched.

Luella was no exception to this power, and by the time the kiss ended she was limp and flushed and gasping for air. Cleo, meanwhile, fought with her own share of emotions, among the fiercest—one she hadn't felt in exactly four years—was envy. The sick, green slime was slowly winding its way through her veins like poison.

Sebastian turned to look at Cleo and she felt even more agitated by his stare. A winged black eyebrow rose in inquiry. "There. Does that suit you, Sister Cleo?" There was no mistaking the mockery in his voice.

Everyone laughed at his words except Haley, who said, "You're always such a jerk, Bas."

Luella was too busy struggling to breathe to even notice.

While Cleo…she was used to his insults. And she had never been frontal about her defense.

This was not the time to do things differently.

She tried unsuccessfully to swallow back a lump of thick saliva stuck in her throat, rendering her speechless. At one point during her college years Cleo had wished she had the balls to tell Sebastian up front what she thought of him and his mockeries, but she was unfortunately a traditional woman, and she had *no* balls.

"I need another vodka," Luella mumbled, still visibly shaken by Sebastian's kiss.

Haley reached for the plush devil toy to spin it once again. Silence befell as they all watched it twirl around and then stop, the tail to Jason, the pitchfork to Haley.

Jason chuckled wickedly, his eyes narrowing at her. "Truth or dare, babe?"

"Dare!" Haley shouted in a burst of enthusiasm.

"That's what I'd hoped." Jason took a swig of his beer and watched her through lowered lashes for several long, endless seconds. "I want you, Haley, very slowly…very gently…to pucker up those lips of yours…bend down…and *kiss my ass, baby*!"

"Eeeew," Haley said, her face contorted with disgust.

Everyone hooted with laughter until Haley stood up and mumbled a curse on her way to where Jason was now standing, midway in the process of dropping his pants.

"You are so gross, Jason," Luella said, and yet out of sheer morbid curiosity, she kept her eyes glued to his pale white buttocks as Haley bent down to kiss them.

The moment Haley pressed her lips to his butt, Jason made a lascivious face. "Oh yeah, yeah, lick it baby, suck it baby, yeah." Haley smacked her hand on the side of his ass to silence him.

Jason's eyes widened. "Hey, I kinda liked that. Can you do it again?"

"You're so funny, Jason," Haley said, all sarcasm as she pulled away from him and headed to sit next to Luella, glowering the whole time. Her cheeks were flushed and though she was scowling, there was an indisputable spark of heat in the depths of her eyes.

"You can't say you didn't like it, Haley," Jason said, the image of solemnity as he zipped up his pants.

"I did not." Haley brushed the back of her hand over her lips to prove it, making Jason laugh.

"You did too."

"If I get to dare you, you're going to have to kiss mine!" she threatened.

"Gee, I would love to."

"Okay, let's keep this shit moving," Luella said, bored already, since she was the kind of person who got extremely bored when she wasn't the center of attention. Before anyone could reply, she spun the devil once more. Cleo swallowed hard when it stopped—the pitchfork staring her in the face, the tail toward Sebastian.

A rope of fear stretched in her insides and coiled around her heart like a noose.

She didn't dare lift her gaze.

"Truth or dare, Cleo?" Sebastian's voice was soft as the breeze itself.

Every time he spoke her name she wondered why it should sound like an indecent proposal. Everything about him, even the way he spoke, distressed her somehow.

"Dare." She didn't think twice. It simply had to be dare. If she opted for truth, he'd want to know private things, personal things, and Cleo would rather die than confess anything about her life to her longtime tormenter.

"Are you sure you want me to dare you, Cleo?"

His voice was low, and Cleo finally forced her gaze to meet his. He was probably enjoying every second of this, the jerk. It seemed like he lived only to taunt and tease her mercilessly, but she couldn't let him know how he affected her. She was certain that casual coolness was the smartest way to go. "Of course. You don't scare me, you big bully," she teased, grateful for the fact that she sounded more convincing than she felt.

His smile was wicked, as if he were enjoying a private little joke. Which she next learned, he actually was.

"I dare you to let me fuck you any way I want to."

Chapter Two

ഔ

Cleo froze for a whole minute, uncertain if he was toying with her or serious. His expression was unreadable, his jaw set firmly. Cleo was certain she heard a thump when her heart dropped to her toes.

"*I'll* fuck you Bas," Luella instantly volunteered.

Sebastian's magnetic black eyes didn't flicker from Cleo's face, now growing whiter by the second. "Thanks baby, but I want Cleo."

At the moment, Cleo's main mission in life was to not die of asphyxiation. Her throat was closed and dry and she felt lightheaded and nauseous from lack of oxygen. She drew in a small little breath while her mind reeled with thoughts. Bad boy, mean-looking, cussing, drinking, whoring Sebastian wanted *her*. He could have — no, he *had* had — every available female, student *and* faculty, on the University of Miami campus. Why he had chosen her as his little private sex toy, not the siren Luella or the spirited Haley, was as inexplicable to Cleo as why her pulse had quickened at his words.

"You're…you're joking," Cleo said when she was finally able to speak. And though she'd hoped it wouldn't, her voice shook drastically. This *had* to be one of thousands of Sebastian's demeaning, not-funny-at-all, revolting little jokes.

"I'm very serious, Cleo."

He said it so calmly, so casually, as if all he had to do was ask and he'd have any woman for the taking. He didn't seem to know for some reason that Cleo was *not* his toy and that she was *not* a whore.

If Cleo wanted to hone her self-assertion skills, now was a good time to do so.

She shook her head firmly, not caring if she was breaking some unmentionable rule of this stupid, silly game. She was not going to participate in anything like this, *especially* if it involved Sebastian Russo. "No," she said.

"No?"

"*No*, Sebastian," she repeated.

Sebastian looked only mildly concerned and with his eyes still fixed on hers, commanded, "Hold her, guys."

The guys obeyed him as if he were the boss of them, as if he were the king and they his subjects, leaving Cleo completely speechless as David clasped one of her wrists and Jason forced the other behind her back. "What are you doing?" she screeched, fighting to free herself, only to have them both none-too-gently lock her arms behind her. Jason winked at her, as if this were all just fun and games. Jason thought *everything* was fun.

"It's no use fighting, Cleo. You wanted a dare. You got it." Rising to his full six feet, two inches of intimidating body mass, Sebastian crossed the circle toward her with a wide, pleased smile on his lips.

"No," Cleo said, trying to break free from her captors. "No. Let me go. This is not funny."

"It's not meant to be funny." Sebastian's voice was dry and humorless.

Wide-eyed, she watched him approach, as big and dark as a shroud of blackness. Cleo felt like a virgin girl about to be sacrificed to the Lord of Hell. He walked toward her deliberately, slowly, as if he wanted to punish her, make her suffer with every step he took. The lone diamond earring he wore in his left ear sparkled blindingly in the lantern light. She wanted to tear it away and fling it at him, see if she could wipe that infernal smirk off his face. Her pulse drummed against her temple, making her head pound, nearly deafening her.

"You've always been a chickenshit, haven't you, Cleo?"

"No, Sebastian," she said firmly, her eyes blazing as she met his steely black gaze.

"Let her go, Bas, she doesn't want you—but don't worry. *I* do," Cleo heard Luella say. Her voice sounded oddly distant, as if Luella were speaking from somewhere else, somewhere far away.

Sebastian's gaze bored into hers, bottomless and fierce. And when he spoke, she knew his words were meant for her only. "Of course she wants me. She's always wanted me."

"That's not true!" Cleo cried.

David snorted beside her and Cleo whipped her face sideways to look at him. "David?" she asked breathlessly.

David shook his head, smiling. "That's bullshit, Cleo," he said.

Jason bent forward to look at her, his eyes sparkling with mirth and lust. "Come on, Cleo baby. You've been at each other's throats for years. Give him a break and just admit it."

"I won't admit anything!" she cried, turning to Sebastian, her chest heaving, her eyes shooting daggers at him. "I won't take my clothes off, Sebastian. I won't do it."

"That's all right. I think I can dispense them without your assistance." With little effort he tore her cotton sundress, ripping the fabric off her body as she cried out a protest and struggled to free herself. From afar, Haley and Luella also protested, too drunk to think coherently or understand the *real* issue here, instead shouting something about expensive women's clothes and how Sebastian ought to pay for that.

When Cleo almost yanked her shoulders out of their sockets from her efforts, she stilled her arms and thrust her legs into the air, kicking wildly, shrieking while Sebastian, deftly avoiding her blows, reached for her panties and tore them off her like paper. Cleo cursed both him *and* his bitch of a mother and he seemed amused by that as he reached for her bra, the last shred of cloth that covered her. The sound of the fabric tearing echoed in the night, until a deathly silence befell and all they could hear were the ragged sounds of Cleo's breathing as she went completely still, fully naked now, her body exposed to the sky and wind like an offering.

"Shit, will you look at the size of those tits!" Jason said beside her.

Gasping for breath, Cleo fought to free herself once more. "Let go of me!" she screeched.

The men yanked her arms farther behind her, their fingers digging into the tender flesh of her wrists as they forcefully stilled her.

Sebastian's eyes roved over her body in a silent caress that heated the insides of her treacherous body like a forest fire running out of control. Her body shook with wanting but Cleo knew better. The last time her body begged for chocolates she'd given in—and ended up red and bloated with allergies for weeks. She wasn't about to listen to its demands now, not now when it had *no* idea what was good for her.

"My God, you're beautiful." Sebastian choked on the words, his gaze greedily absorbing every detail of her body. She could swear his eyes touched her, for she could feel them brushing over her hot, fevered skin with the gentleness of a feather.

Beside her, David and Jason looked at their leisure, their gazes shining with lust at the sight of her ripe, round breasts.

"I could suck those babies forever," Jason mumbled.

"Sebastian," Cleo begged softly, her eyes pleading with his. "Please don't."

Something flickered in his eyes, something dark and haunting. "Save the begging for later, beautiful. And stand up so I can look my fill."

"No!" she squealed, even as she was hauled upright by her captors.

Cleo felt her legs tremble beneath her and found she could only remain on her feet because of David's and Jason's support. Sebastian circled her, his eyes missing nothing. She yelped when he slapped a hand to her buttock, bouncing her muscle with the hit and making her skin sting afterward.

"Hmm. Nice."

He smacked her other buttock with a harsh slap and she bit her lower lip to muffle the whimper that came. His finger dipped into the crevice between her cheeks, up and down, slowly following the curve of her rump, and Cleo swore she would faint.

Then Sebastian resumed his circling once again, his steps painfully slow as he walked around her.

Cleo's eyes landed on the plush red devil that lay untouched on the sand a few feet away from her. It was as if the thing had possessed them. That harmless little toy had turned this game into a nightmare.

"Look at me."

Cleo gritted her teeth, refusing to look at Sebastian, instead keeping her gaze fixed on the toy devil, the least menacing of the two. At least *that* devil wasn't a hypocrite. At least that devil carried its pitchfork and tail and didn't pretend to be something it wasn't, while Sebastian sometimes did, and it was cruel.

Cleo remembered many times—too many to forget, even though she'd tried—when Sebastian had been good to her. He'd hugged her when she'd missed an exam, kissed her temple oh-so softly. Studying had been of utmost importance to Cleo and he'd occasionally let her cry about her college tragedies in the comfort of his arms. And yet after every one of these surprising, unexpected moments, he would transform in the blink of an eye and become…mean. He would then mock her, tease her, sneer at her, making the memories of those too-brief tender moments as painful as his taunts.

He'd even danced with her once. Sebastian despised dancing, but he'd done so because she was the only girl at the party sitting down lonely and with a lump in her throat…

When the song started, Cleo held Sebastion nearly at arm's length, keeping a safe distance between them, like she'd do with anyone else. But he wasn't anyone else. He was Sebastian Russo, and he immediately protested, a low vibration rumbling in his chest as he grabbed her waist and pulled her forward. "Please don't, Bas," Cleo said shakily, but he pressed her to him anyway, despite the slight push of her palms at his shoulders.

He was taller by at least a head, and far bigger and stronger. His grip was not in the least bit gentle and she shouldn't have been aroused by the harsh, possessive way he held her waist. But it did arouse her. Uncomfortably, embarrassingly so.

Cleo kept her eyes averted, taking care to look at the couples dancing beside them instead. Just being near him made her feel needy and she had to check back the impulse to cling to his massive, hard male body as it soothingly rocked against hers.

"Put your arms around me, Cleo," she heard him say. His voice, so near, so husky, moved her more than any love song ever could. It made her sex tingle and for that disturbing feeling alone, she locked her arms straight and pushed back slightly, needing to put more space between them. Space to breathe.

"I'm fine, thank you," she said, keeping her arms stiff on his shoulders, her eyes roaming. "Thanks for dancing with me. I know you didn't really want to."

"Stop looking at everyone else and look at me."

Cleo had to quickly come up with a plausible excuse for avoiding his gaze, so she said, "I was just wondering where Luella and Haley are. Do you see them?" Glancing past his shoulder, she busily studied the crowd.

"Cleo." Lean, muscled arms slid around her waist, yanking her body closer to his at the same time he bent his head and whispered, "Come here."

At the unexpected flood in her panties and the sudden racing of her heart, Cleo's instincts told her to step back. When she tried, his arms tightened around her, causing all sorts of whirlwinds inside her while she kept her eyes away from his face and her palms pushing at his chest. She started to babble. "Look, there's Mrs. Schmidt—did you ever take classes with her? She's such a good teacher...but I don't think I see Luella or Haley anywhere. Where could they be?"

Every muscle in his body suddenly turned to stone and he stopped dancing completely. "It's no fucking wonder no one wants to dance with you, Cleo."

He said it so stiffly his lips hardly moved when he spoke. Cleo didn't know why he should be angry – she'd been nothing but nice. She was always nothing but nice to him.

She stared at his lips, her stomach clenching horribly. "Why do you always have to insult me, Bas?" she whispered, hating that her voice broke.

He gripped her chin and forced her to meet his gaze, his eyes glowing with anger. "Go and find your friends."

Cursing under his breath, he left her alone in the middle of the dance floor and headed off to dance with another. With a woman Cleo hated right then and there, a whore he fairly made love to on the dance floor, right in front of her eyes. And his eyes sought out hers in a silent dare, in defiance, as the woman rubbed her scantily clad body against his very notorious erection. His eyes, those cruel, piercing black eyes, remained fixed on Cleo as he roamed his hands freely over inches and inches of soft, supple female flesh. Those same strong, calloused hands that only moments ago had touched and melted her suddenly cupped that whore's rump and pressed her to him, his beautiful dark head bending forward as his thick, magnificent lips swooped down to capture hers.

Cleo had wanted to die.

"I said *look at me*, Cleo."

Cleo's mind snapped back to the present. How many times had he spoken those very same words to her? Dozens, maybe even hundreds of times. She was certain if he asked her to disappear completely it would have been a far easier request.

Gathering her courage, she slowly looked up at him and shuddered at the darkness of his eyes. The flickering lantern light from below etched his features into hard planes of light and shadows. He looked unyielding and vicious and frightening.

"You should have chosen truth."

Cleo drew in a deep, audible breath at the direct contact of his hand on her skin when he cupped her hip. "But I'm glad you didn't." He slid his hand up to her ribs and ran his thumb along the bottom curve of her breast. "You're really going to get it this time, Cleo." His free hand grasped her jaw, his thumb and fingers digging into her cheeks as he squeezed, forcing her lips into a pout. "And you're going to get it from *me*."

He sounded crazed, angry—desperate.

He kissed her forcibly, his lips covering the plump flesh of her pouted lips, kept open only by the force of his grip on her cheeks. He thrust his tongue inside her mouth and Cleo swayed backward, only to be steadied by a pair of hands on her elbows. His tongue ravaged her, and when she heard the sounds of his deep, haggard breathing, she knew with frightening certainty that one way or another he would take her tonight. The thought made her heart leap, whether in fright or inexplicable thrill, she didn't know.

Sebastian pulled away from her, panting hard and visibly straining to recover.

For many reasons—one very important one in particular—Cleo wanted to scream at him. She'd never done anything to him, had never done anything to anyone. Why did he hate her? Why did he want to punish her, hurt her?

She'd *loved* him, damn him. Desperately so. Despite how he'd hurt her, humiliated her, laughed at her. It shamed her to admit it, even to herself. It had taken her almost four years to forget him, to pick up the pieces of her battered, sorry little heart.

"Lie down, Mother Cleo," he sneered, slamming his eyes into lethal slits. "And open your legs."

Cleo knew that begging him would be like fueling his hatred, nurturing this sick, festered need of his to humiliate her. So instead she turned to Jason, met his deep blue eyes with her own.

"Jason please…let me go."

"It's just a game Cleo, just relax," Jason said with a smile.

"No, it's not!" she yelled.

She turned to David, her former study companion and one of only two men in her entire life who'd held her naked in his arms. "David, please!"

David's dark brown eyes slowly studied her features. "I'll stop this, Cleo. If you really mean it, I will. But we both know you don't, do you?"

Cleo lowered her eyelashes, not bearing to look at him. David knew, of course. He *knew*. That last night in college, Cleo had spoken someone else's name when David had made love to her. It had been just a whisper, almost painful to speak aloud, but by the way he had stiffened she knew he had heard it clearly. Cleo was *still* embarrassed about it, and she still wanted to believe she hadn't spoken that name out loud in an intimate moment.

Her voice broke. "David, I just—"

"Zip it you three!" Sebastian thundered. "Sit down and open your legs for me, Cleo. I'm coming in…and I'm coming inside you."

"You bastard!" she screeched furiously, wanting to rip his eyes out, but Jason and David held back her wrists and pulled her downward, forcing her to sit on a blanket.

Sebastian chuckled a slow, mirthless laugh. His laugh sounded old, as if it had rusted from so little use.

Slowly kneeling before her, he placed his hand over her knee. She jerked at his touch, her heart pounding against her breast like a mad little thing. Splaying his fingers over her knee, he slid his hand upward, shifting his thumb to her inner thigh. His touch was firm, possessive. It scorched her, *all* of her, even her heart, as if he'd taken what was left of it and flung it into the fiery red pit of a volcano.

She knew he should make her sick. She *knew* she should cringe at his touch, but instead her body felt like liquid. Like she had wings to fly and was floating above the ground as if by magic. Still she despised it, despised the way he made her feel and the hundreds of times he'd made her cry. So she slammed her legs shut, trapping his wayward hand in the process.

He shook his head, a lock of black hair falling on his forehead when he did so. "If I didn't know better, I'd think you didn't want me."

"I don't."

"Liar."

With both hands and with little effort, he forced her thighs open. She yelped when he cupped her pussy, splaying his fingers on her ass and rubbing the heel of his palm against her clit. His touch ignited her. Closing her eyes, she mewled helplessly as she fought the wildness raging inside her.

"You're very aroused, Cleo. So wet. You've made it a habit of lying to yourself all these years."

"I don't…lie. Please stop…*stop* this."

"Do you really want me to stop?"

It was hard to look at him. Hard to look at his proud, powerful face, but she forced herself to. Bravely, she opened her eyes and met his lethal black gaze, biting her lower lip in a futile attempt to keep it from trembling. It wasn't fair that he should know. Know how and where to touch her, to bend her will in such a way. "Yes."

That shaky word brought a well of stinging tears to her eyes and she quickly dropped her eyelashes to hide them from him. There was no way in hell she was ever going to admit that she wanted him. No way in hell would she ever succumb to his caresses, to his domination, no matter what her body wanted. No matter what her heart said. The poor thing was badly broken and poorly mended. The little dear obviously had no idea what it was in for if she succumbed. It was *not* in its best interest and she would not willingly put herself through four more years of misery.

She swallowed the lump in her throat and drew in a deep breath. She wouldn't let him see her cry. Why *should* she cry? All she had to do was say no and mean it, and this would be over with. Sebastian might be the meanest son of a bitch in the world but her friends—no matter how far gone and drunk—would never allow him to hurt her. And deep down, Cleo knew it.

"What is this?" Sebastian whispered, his breath hot against her face as he bent forward. She would have preferred he mock her, for the concern in his voice was even more painful. His thumbs brushed the wetness from the corners of her eyes. "Are you crying, Cleo?"

Cleo forced her eyes open with the last remaining shreds of hostility she'd clung to like a lifesaver. "I hate you," she hissed.

The men's grips tightened around her wrists when she tried to pull away but her movements were weak, as if she'd been somehow drained of all energy. She tried once again but before even making a decent effort, went limp in defeat. Maybe it was better to stop fighting so he could finish with her already—finish the slow, painful torment he'd subjected her to for years. Perhaps when he was through she might not feel *anything* anymore. Maybe this overwhelming hate for him would be replaced by nothing but a welcome, blissful numbness.

"Baby...I want to make you shudder and scream and moan. I don't want you to cry." He cupped her face with his big, strong hands and brushed his lips against hers. Cleo lost her breath completely when he pressed his lips to hers firmly and forced his tongue into her mouth.

Fire. She was on fire...blazing under the strokes of his strong, wet tongue.

Heat flamed inside her like a furnace and he fed it with every thrust, every dark claim of his tongue. He pillaged her lips, claimed every inch of her as his own. She fell under his spell, his black magic, and even moaned when he tilted his head sideways to gain better access. He tasted of things that were hazardous, bad for your health—beer and cigarettes and man. It couldn't be good for her, feeling this. It couldn't be good for her, wanting him. All of him. All the time.

When he withdrew, Cleo was feverish and breathing harshly.

"Why don't I give you a few minutes to think about it?" Sebastian calmly suggested, seemingly unaffected by the same kiss that had left her limp, dazed and burning.

Chapter Three

۞

Cleo shuddered when he left her, suddenly feeling cold and vulnerable, her chest heaving with each breath, her eyes wild and desperate on his retreating back.

For a crazy moment she would now promptly forget, she wanted to beg him to come back to her. Beg him to touch her, fuck her. Beg him to break the strict, self-imposed restrictions she'd lived with her whole life and make loud, crazy love to her like he had to the women who'd stumbled out of his dorm room after hours and hours of moaning. Instead, she silently watched as he paused before Luella and stretched a hand out to her, palm up.

"Let's show Cleo how it's done, shall we?"

"With you? Are you kidding me? I've *lived* for this moment."

There was a sharp spark of desperation in Cleo's eyes as she watched Luella daintily set her hand in his bigger one. He lifted her to her feet with an effortless tug and with slow, precise movements that meant he did this sort of thing very often—more often than Cleo would like to know—began to remove Luella's clothing.

He pulled the pink cotton top over her head then kissed her lips while his hands worked on the button of her tight blue jeans. Luella wore no bra, and her breasts heaved as she bent and helped him undress her. Her jeans dropped to her ankles with a soft *whoosh*. Standing in all her splendor, wearing only a flimsy pair of panties, Luella stepped out of her jeans and toward the glorious man before her.

"Nice," Sebastian whispered, eyeing her appreciatively.

Luella moaned when his hand disappeared into the soft silk fabric of her panties. Cleo's throat went dry, and although the hold of the men beside her had slackened around her wrists, she was too engrossed in the scene unfolding to even notice.

"You're so wet, so slippery, baby," Sebastian said in a hot, husky voice.

Luella's answer was a deep, loud moan and a thrust of her hips against Sebastian's probing hand.

"Bas, please," Luella begged, rubbing her breasts against his chest and rocking her pelvis against the onslaught of his hand.

"In a moment, sweetheart…but first things first."

He took Luella's shoulders and turned her around to face Cleo. He stood behind her, a whole head taller than she was, and Cleo was helpless but to watch the slow movement of his lips as they grazed Luella's earlobe while his hands cupped her breasts from behind. His fingers were long and tapered, his hands big and sleek, easily managing to cup the whole flesh of Luella's perfect silicone breasts.

"Do you see this, Cleo?" he asked softly, his eyes boring into hers. His thumbs ran circles around Luella's areolas. "This is what I want to do to you."

He buried his face in Luella's neck and nuzzled it with his lips while one of his hands traveled down past her navel, sinking into her panties once again. Cleo could clearly see the movement of his finger beneath the shimmering white fabric. It rose and stretched as the lean limb of his finger slowly thrust inside her. Moaning, Luella threw her head back, her long blonde-streaked hair falling over Sebastian's shoulder.

"See, Cleo? She likes it. So will you."

Cleo's energy was now solely directed into fighting the wild, consuming ardor burning inside her. She met Sebastian's compelling black eyes and remained silent as she watched him slowly pull away from Luella and begin to undress. She could feel his gaze engulfing her, slowly shredding away her decency, her morale, until everything she felt was nothing short of animal.

"Take off your panties, sweetheart," he uttered to Luella.

In her hurry, Luella was faster than he was, flushed and eager to be taken by him, while Sebastian took his time. When Cleo finally saw him fully naked, his clothes discarded over the sand, she swore she hated him more than ever before.

He was perfection, as tempting as sin itself. His was a body worthy of a centerfold, no airbrushing needed, no cropping or pasting. Just as he was. Tall, lean and muscled. His skin was tight over his muscles and deeply tanned, gleaming against the flickering lanterns like polished gold. Cleo all but gaped at the curves of his biceps and arms, the hardness of his pectorals, the lean, muscled valley of his stomach.

And then his cock, standing tall and proud from a mat of hair as dark as his eyes. It was a weapon, one used to claim and conquer, and to have the honor of sheltering it, to sheathe and nurture it, had to be in its very own way a small piece of heaven. Cleo remembered thinking of it, dreaming of it, wanting it madly and to no reason.

She hadn't *wanted* to want him. Of the hundreds of men she'd met in her life, Sebastian was the last man she'd ever wanted to fall for. He was everything she'd been taught to avoid, everything she'd stayed away from her whole life. There was nothing honorable about him.

If only her body would listen.

Suddenly Haley joined them. When Sebastian cupped Luella's hips from behind and slid his cock inside her, Haley knelt behind him, lowered herself between his long, powerful legs and slowly began to suck on the big, heavy balls dangling temptingly above her.

"Whatever you do, Haley baby, don't stop," Sebastian said in a low, raspy voice, his words earning him a soft little moan and a long, thorough lick to the balls from the eager Haley, who'd closed her eyes and was kissing and nipping his sac like a starved person. As if suffering from a deadly fever, Luella bent forward and brusquely shoved back her ass to receive his length completely.

For some reason Cleo was simply not aware of, Sebastian's eyes never left her. Even when she'd been absorbed studying every inch of his naked body, she'd felt his piercing black eyes on her. And now, as he rhythmically slid his throbbing cock inside Luella, shoving his hips against her buttocks and making her breasts bounce from the force of his thrusts while Haley pleased him from underneath, he had eyes only for Cleo.

She couldn't stand it, the heat of his gaze, the dark proposal in it.

Cleo closed her eyes to block the image but when she did, she found that the sight of Sebastian taking Luella from behind had been indelibly branded onto her retinas. Luella screamed like a she-cat and Cleo found little comfort in the pitch-blackness of her closed eyelids, for it was impossible to block their sounds. Her brain conjured up images as she listened to Sebastian's harsh, deep breaths, Luella's hussy little moans and Haley's low, savoring whimpers.

A moan tore from Cleo's chest when a pair of lips closed around her nipple. Her eyes opened to find David bending to take the other nipple into his mouth while Jason licked and suckled the one he'd found first. Jason groaned in agony, as if he were in a terrible amount of pain, and then she realized he'd pulled out his dick and was slowly stroking himself.

Cleo felt her sex tighten at the onslaught. Two tongues circling her nipples, two hungry mouths suckling her breasts.

"Do you like this, Cleo?" David murmured against the flesh of her breast. "Would you like us to kiss you? Pleasure you?"

She whimpered in answer and at the deep wanton sound, they both groaned, the vibrations on her flesh sending waves of pleasure through her body in torrents.

Her eyes fell on Sebastian's powerful form, his hips slamming against Luella's buttocks while she yelped in heat and need and want. Haley was now cupping his buttocks and grazing the thin skin of his balls with her teeth, slightly tugging, and Cleo watched Sebastian close his eyes and groan deep with pleasure.

She used to get both captured and enraged when she'd watched him simply kiss someone. Now, watching him with two women while she sat there naked, waiting like a captive for him to come to her, felt like dying. A war raged within her, desire, jealousy, hate and want collided and fought, made her whimper in frustration, desperation. Her sex clenched with desire while her soul seemed to shatter into a thousand pieces.

"Can I put my dick on your tits baby?" Jason asked, his voice thick and urgent as he stroked himself.

"Yes," she found herself saying in a low, sultry voice.

Yes, because she was crazy and angry and burning. Yes, because she wanted to hurt Sebastian Russo, hurt him like he was hurting her right now, torturing her as he had sex with the other women. Loving them. Touching them. Just like in college.

David moved behind her and nuzzled her earlobe while Jason positioned himself in front of her and gently guided his cock to her breasts with a raw, frenzied look of ecstasy.

"I'm not going to hurt you, Cleo. I just want to rub my dick…here." Cupping the sides of her full, heavy breasts, he pressed them together while he thrust his dick between them with slow, deliberate strokes. "You've got awesome tits, Cleo. They feel so good around my cock, so soft and big. Oh…baby…oh *shit*."

Cleo felt feverish, aroused at the thought of Sebastian seeing her like this, of making him feel the rage, the hatred, the desperation she felt in watching him do what he was doing. She'd been watching him fondle and kiss other women for years—dying slowly each time.

"Yes…*yes, Jason*!" Cleo urged—and then she knew. Could feel it as certain as she felt her own pulse—Sebastian was watching. He was watching Jason as he rocked above her, whispering praises to her as he fondled and fucked her breasts, and all she could hope for—pray for—was that he would feel even a trace of the sheer, destructive pain he made her feel.

Thrusting faster, Jason groaned and pressed her breasts tighter together. Leaning back against David's chest, Cleo could feel his gaze burn the top of her head as he watched in fascination the way Jason's erect cock fairly disappeared between the huge mountains of her breasts.

"Your tits…so amazing…so soft…so damned *huge*…" Jason whispered. He looked down at her with ravaged blue eyes. "I wanna come, Cleo. I wanna come on your tits."

The carnal look in his eyes sent a spark of heat from her sex to every nerve in her body like a thunderbolt. She trembled slightly and arched her back as Jason pumped his hips and shuddered over her, shooting his semen in several thick, creamy spurts just above her breasts. His come was warm when it spilled and dribbled down her skin, trailing a shiny path toward her nipples.

"Lick it baby," he breathed, still shuddering slightly and rocking his hips in slow, receding efforts.

For some ungodly reason she did as he asked. She pushed up her breasts and licked her skin, her own sweat and his semen. Jason plopped down to her side, his movement revealing Sebastian's gaze, hot and livid on her. Under his watch, Cleo made an art of licking Jason's semen with the tip of her tongue, drawing it into her mouth ever so slowly, as if it were a banquet. It was salty, warm, with a musky scent that filled her nostrils.

Sebastian's expression was that of an enraged, lustful demon as he watched her, narrow-eyed, his hands fisting over Luella's hips. He was ramming into her like a primitive beast, the tight, sinewy muscles of his arms and legs rippling as he did so. Only seconds after Luella shuddered beneath him did he walk toward Cleo, his cock glistening from Luella's juices and straining up toward the sky in defiance.

"Cleo's mine, fucking jerk-offs. Find yourselves another partner," he snapped.

David and Jason scrambled across the sand and Sebastian's eyes fell to the distended crests of her nipples, shining with both men's kisses and Jason's semen.

Growling low in his throat, he dropped to his knees before her, cupping her breasts in his hands and brushing his thumbs over the wetness, erasing their marks. Braced back on her elbows, Cleo was no longer being held down except by the force of his fierce black gaze, and she found it was just as efficient.

She swore she hated him, and how she could hate him so powerfully when she'd loved him so deeply and wanted him so much was a mystery she would probably never in her life understand.

Gathering saliva, she spit at him, sent it splattering to his face. Snarling, he narrowed his eyes, bending forward so that his bared teeth were only an inch away from her face. "You'll regret that, Cleo." Just as quickly he spat at her pussy, and she jerked at the impact of his saliva against her swollen labia and clit. Pressing his hands against her shoulders, he brutally forced her down on the sand.

"Let me go," she hissed with more force than she thought she could manage.

"If you want to play the coy little virgin girl, that's fine with me. I'm fucking you anyway."

Lowering her voice to a mere whisper, she searched his face with wide, cautious eyes. "Why are you doing this?"

"Because I want to."

She gritted her teeth. "Just because you *want* and you *can* do something doesn't mean you *should*!"

His fingers dug into her shoulders. "Is that what's kept you from my bed all these years?"

"That, yes! And the fact that you're a vicious, rude, crude, nasty gigolo!"

"Maybe if you'd given me some of this I wouldn't have had to sleep with half the town, baby," he gritted, cupping her cunt in his palm and brusquely rubbing in his saliva.

Cleo stiffened at the touch, biting back a moan.

When the pad of his thumb scraped over her clit, a scorching heat, swift and blinding, surged through her body in shock waves. She fought to still it, control it, tensing her muscles as it unleashed. Sebastian's thick lips were an inch from hers and when he spoke, the scent of beer wafted to her nostrils, dizzying her. "I'll bet your pussy is sweeter than any I've ever tasted before."

"No," she breathed. "You're mean. You're a *devil*, Sebastian."

"Yes, I am. And I've been in hell because of you." He parted her legs farther and shoved his hard chest between her thighs, gazing down at her swollen sex with hot, heavy eyes. "You're so horny I can smell you, Cleo—it makes me want to eat you." Her cunt flooded with desire when he bent and grazed her curls with his lips. Then, ever so slowly, he flicked his tongue and licked her clit with a single deep stroke.

It was hell.

"Sebastian, please don't…"

Don't do this or don't stop? she vaguely wondered. His touch felt so good yet at the same time, so very painful. She couldn't think, couldn't concentrate…could only feel. His swift, powerful tongue was now spearing inside her creamy pussy like a sword, killing her resistance with each thrust.

"Quit the chat and fuck her, Bas," Jason called from behind. "Fuck those tits, man!"

"Yeah, we want to hear Cleo moan. Time to loosen up, Cleo sweetie," Haley offered cheerily. "The time has *come* for you to *come*!"

Sebastian growled between her legs, not liking the intrusion of their voices, not a man who appreciated being told what to do. But his tongue remained, delving inside her and Cleo thought she'd die from the shame. She was ashamed that she was enjoying this, ashamed to admit that, yes, she'd always—*always*—wanted this man. Inside her. Fucking. Taking. Cursing. Biting.

She'd envied those women. Those loose women he always accessorized with, one on each arm, each exposing an ample share of cleavage and legs.

Cleo had been jealous but she'd swiftly smothered the feeling, telling herself repeatedly those women were whores, hussies and sluts. They had no brains and were valued solely for their bodies. Cleo frequently found herself thinking how she should pity those poor, lost creatures, and how she—Cleo Sonterra—was worth more than that, more than just a sexy body, for she had a beautiful soul. She was a giving person, intelligent and dedicated. She was worth more than those whores, more than those women who got to feel Sebastian's hands on their naked bodies, more than those women who got to be held in a limp hypnosis in his sleek, muscled arms. Cleo wasn't worthless because Sebastian didn't want her, didn't love her back. His lack of want didn't make her worthless. It just made him mean and stupid.

Because Cleo had loved him more than anyone *ever* possibly could.

She didn't love him anymore—she couldn't. Not after he'd crushed her heart repeatedly and rendered it incapable of such an emotion.

She didn't even *like* him.

He had no scruples. He was a beast who broke women's hearts with no regard to their feelings. Lying, cheating, stealing — he did it all for the hell of it. His laugh was always cynical and he constantly cursed the world and everything in it. He was not a man she would *ever* introduce to her parents.

Yet she'd wanted him, *still* wanted him. And perhaps more than fear him, she feared her desire, for it was wild and untamed and dangerous. And it was always there. Always this longing, this wanting.

Him. Sebastian Russo. The meanest son of a bitch who ever lived.

Chapter Four

∞

Sebastian groaned at the feel of her body, plush, pliant and shivering beneath him. This was all he'd wanted throughout his college years and every single minute of his life afterward, and though it might have been a rough way to go about it, hell—he was drunk, he was horny and he wanted *her*. Cleo.

Her sweet pink cunt tasted like heaven to his lips. The juices spilling from her vagina all but flowed into his mouth and her muscles tightened wantonly around his tongue as he buried it deep inside her.

Growling, he cupped her buttocks and lifted her hips higher to have better access to that sweet, tight pussy he'd so often ached to taste. She rewarded him with a soft little yelp. The sound reverberated in his insides like a penance, sending a jolt of red-hot lightning to his dick.

She no longer fought him. She was now as limp and pliant as a rag doll, and yet she was hot to the touch, sweaty with the heat of her desire. It had been useless for her to fight him anymore, just as it had been useless for him to fight this inexplicable madness of wanting her.

He'd thought four years would be enough to get her image out of his mind but instead he'd been tortured, nearly gone crazy over not being able to look at her, even if just to tease and torment her.

It bugged him—*she* bugged him. At every gathering during their college years she'd hardly looked at him, hardly recognized his presence, as if he were unworthy of her precious attentions. He'd sworn to himself he'd seduce her, only to realize she was immune to him, pushing his hand back when it strayed, jerking her eyes away when he looked at her with lust and thinking he was mocking her whenever he spoke one of his very rare, very sparse compliments.

All she'd done was ignore him. Brutally so. And like a brat wanting Mommy to look his way, he'd misbehaved, wanting her to turn, to look, even if just to wrinkle her perfect button nose at him. And yet not even to do *that* would she spare him a glance.

Even though he knew with painful certainty that she absolutely, irrefutably hated his guts, she still wanted him. By God, she did. He'd be damned if he'd misinterpreted the dewy-eyed look she'd been sending his way tonight. It was a look filled with lust and years and years of wanting. He recognized a goddamned look like that when he saw one. And by God, he'd fuck her. He'd fuck her whether she wanted him to or not. He was way past caring now. All he cared about was possessing, marking her as his own, and if wanting her like this made him the devil himself, so be it.

He heard sounds behind him—a man's low growl, a woman's soft whimpering—and he imagined his friends were already screwing their drunken brains out. He didn't give a shit who was fucking who and how. All he gave a damn about was the little piece of ass he had in his hands and the cunt he was eating from, which was about the best-tasting pussy he'd had in his life. Her flavor was spicy, and it was hot and scorching on his tongue, making it tingle after a taste.

He lifted his face and looked into her eyes. Those eerie doe eyes were clouded with lust and her breasts heaved heavily with every breath she took. She had the biggest breasts he'd ever seen. Round and full, with small, perky nipples in such a soft shade of pink they almost blended with her skin. She'd been a fool to think she could hide those tits from him with those ridiculous loose dresses she wore. She'd all but made them look bigger, saucier...more enticing.

He ran his hands along her hips and up to cup that tiny little waist. Her skin was as soft as churned butter, and how that little waist could properly carry the weight of her breasts was beyond him. When his hands cupped those huge, melon-sized fruits he growled with delight. They filled his hands, overflowed his fingers, and her puckered nipples brushed against his palms, begging for attention.

He moved up to draw one perky crest into his mouth and sucked it full force, making her whimper. He sank his teeth into her skin and bit her fiercely while he sucked. He wanted to mark those breasts as *his*, and if he drew blood, so be it. She cried out, sinking her fingers into his hair, pulling him closer.

He didn't need more encouragement than that.

Snarling, he squeezed her other breast with his hand until she whimpered, her nipple taut and hard and ready. Shifting his attention, he drew the hard little pebble into his mouth and sank his teeth around it while he sucked. She screamed beneath him, a scream filled with pain and pleasure and loud enough to echo in the sky.

Sebastian felt drugged and out of control and for some unholy, sick reason, he needed to hear her whimper and moan, harder, louder, be it from pleasure or pain or both. God knows he, too, was feeling both. It was painful to touch her, painful to have watched others touch her, brutally so.

"You shouldn't have let Jason touch you," he breathed as he gazed down at her with hot, lustful eyes. Her lips were wet and swollen, and the amber specks in her chocolate-brown eyes glimmered like gold in the night.

"He asked me nicer than you did," she said breathlessly.

Grinding his teeth, he squeezed her breasts so hard they could have exploded in his hands. "I've taken all the shit from you I can take. Now you're going to admit it."

"Admit what?"

"That you're a fucking little bitch and all you've wanted is for me to fuck you."

"No."

"Say it, damn you!"

"What do you want me to say?" she screamed in desperation.

Growling, he moved forward so that his face was a breath from hers. "I want you to say you want this. I want you to admit you want *me*."

She was panting hard beneath him, her eyes fevered and her lips trembling as she gazed up at him. The rise and fall of her breasts drew his eyes and he gazed down at them in ownership, at the red marks his mouth had left and the slightly indented marks of his teeth. Her creamy skin gleamed with a fine sheen of sweat and he ached to lick it…lick her everywhere.

There were so many things he wanted to do to her. And yet he couldn't stand the pressure in his cock, the pain in his balls. If he couldn't think straight, it was because every drop of blood in his body was settled between his legs and pulsing wildly in his cock. He ached to bury it deep inside her and fuck her until he bled from the effort.

"Please, Bas…" she whispered softly.

Pulling back slightly, he scowled down at her, furious at the way the plea in her voice tugged at his insides. He'd be damned before he let that tiny, pleading little voice of hers get to him. He'd be damned before she convinced him to switch from fucking her to cuddling before a fireplace and eating bonbons while they chatted the night away. All he wanted to do, all he'd *ever* wanted to do, was take her, claim her, fuck her. He was not stopping now, not even if that voice yanked at his heartstrings and strangled him with them. "I'm not stopping, Cleo. Whether you like it or not, you're mine tonight."

"You're…hurting me," she whimpered softly.

"I'm not even touching you."

She shook her head, specks of runaway sand glittering in her hair. "You're *killing* me."

The hell he was. He framed her face with his hands and looked deep into her heavy-lidded gaze. "No. You're killing *me*."

Cleo clutched him tightly, fisting her hands in the thick mass of his hair. "*Sebastian...*"

He heard the need in her voice, low and clear and beautiful, and it robbed him of his breath completely.

There was a deathly silence while he slowly raked her face with his eyes, attempting to memorize those sweet, wholesome features which now, sweaty and hot and needy, were the most beautiful he'd ever seen.

"You want me." It was a whispered statement, delivered with more confidence than he felt. His heartbeat seemed to completely stop as he waited for her answer.

It was just a breath but he heard it. Heard it while he watched her plush pink lips form the words he'd waited years to hear.

"God help me, I do."

He'd dreamed of this moment. He'd dreamed of prim and proper Miss Cleo begging him to fuck her. In his wildest dreams she'd yelled, "Screw me, fuck me, you bastard, please!" but he supposed he would settle for anything. As long as it meant screwing, fucking, mating — her.

His lips crushed hers with shattering force, sending shudders all through her body in shock waves. A soft little whimper escaped her lips but the sound was barely audible as he muffled it with his mouth.

Behind them someone was coming, and coming hard, their shouts high and mighty as they reached their climax.

The sounds invigorated Sebastian, inviting him to seek his own release, release inside *her*, inside this woman — this reluctant little bitch. Feeling her pliant, soft body beneath his and the warmth of her skin seared him, burned his soul like a stake right through the heart.

He kissed her fiercely while a finger ambled down her stomach until it sank into the glorious place it sought—the tight, wet sheath of her pussy. She was swollen with need and the walls of her cunt clenched around his finger and sucked it in like a magnet. He was sweating profusely and every gleaming inch of his body was tense and burning for her. He wanted to sink his cock inside her and spill himself, mark her as his, but at the same time he didn't want this to end. He wanted her now—now and always.

"You feel so tight, like a little virgin, Cleo."

The words were breathed against her lips as he slid another finger inside her, stretching her walls to accommodate both. She was tight, slippery. Jerking his wrist, he screwed both fingers inside until she arched her back and moaned in pleasure. The feel of her nipples brushing against his naked chest tore a curse from his lips.

Cleo shifted her hips, wanting his hardness to fill her, but he caught her pelvis with his hand and stilled her. If she'd inched her pussy even a hair closer to his cock he'd be buried deep inside her and spilling his semen within seconds, and he wanted to take his time. He'd already waited a lifetime for this moment. He'd be damned if he didn't make it last.

She exceeded even his wildest, wettest dreams—which had been plentiful, and all of them starring little Miss Cleo. Soft, pliant and womanly, with a body fit for a porn star, a body that, just looking at it, made a man want to jerk off and come. This was Cleo, and she was moaning under him, her tongue kissing his mouth like a hungry—no, *starved*—little slut who hadn't had an orgasm in years.

Sebastian would be more than happy to oblige. He'd make her come like she'd never, ever come before. While he was going to come everywhere, make sure every inch of her plush little body had *his* mark. So that if he never had the fortune of touching her again, she would at least remember this forever—remember *him* forever.

Chapter Five

ॐ

He touched her slowly, his fingers sliding in and out of her pussy with a mind-jerking lack of haste that drove her mad. She protested with a weak whimper and lifted her hips to meet his movements. Wanting more, needing more.

"You're begging for it, aren't you, Cleo?" His voice was gruff and thick with lust. He dragged his body downward, took her knees and bent them until her legs were completely folded, her knees touching her shoulders, her sex wet and pink and open to him. She panicked, tried to straighten her legs but he halted her.

"Let me look at you, Cleo. Don't move." His eyes glazed and burned with desire when he spread the labia of her sex open with two fingers and stared right into her.

She bucked with shamefulness, feeling exposed and vulnerable, but he shushed her with softly spoken, unintelligible words, gently keeping the folds open as he bent down to lick her. He drank her up as if he were in the middle of the desert and she were an oasis. Thirsty, starved, like a man gone mad.

Her toes curled with tension when a long, probing finger sank slowly into the tight back entrance of her ass. Cleo jerked from the intrusion, suddenly realizing the helpless, pitiful yelping sounds reverberating in the air were coming from her.

The combination of his finger—now slowly stroking the puckered entrance of her ass in gentle, teasing circles—and the merciless thrusts of his tongue on her oozing sex could have been enough to kill her. But she held on for dear, dear life, wanting and needing to find out what other things—bad things, good things, *any* things—he planned to do to her. It was heaven, it was hell and it was all she wanted. All she'd ever wanted. Him. Loving her. Touching her. Kissing her.

Fucking her.

He groaned low and deep in his throat, indicating with that painfully sensual sound that the excruciating pleasure Cleo felt in receiving was similar to what he experienced in giving. An ache to please him, to see his face straining with desire like it had been when Haley licked him as he took Luella from behind, burned inside her like a death wish.

Suddenly switching places, his tongue traveled lower to kiss the rosette of her ass while one of the fingers that had kept her swollen labia parted now slid deeply inside her. One finger then became two, and two became three, until his fingers spread her cunt in a way she thought would make her burst. A tension unlike any other coiled in the pit of her being and though she thought it impossible, the tension tightened further at each thrust, each touch, each kiss. She writhed as he slowly kissed and licked her ass, first teasing her with his lips then using his powerful, wet tongue.

"I can't stand this, Bas," she breathed, lifting her head to look at him.

But he was buried between her legs and all she could see was the silky black mane of hair at the top of his head as he cocked it sideways to continue his conquest. Before Cleo fell back against the sand, she caught a quick glance of her friends watching in a stupor as Sebastian made wild, sweet, bad love to her.

She wasn't ashamed now…now the only thing that mattered was Sebastian.

She could have sworn she was a breath away from reaching that point, that point where all was lost to her for an infinitesimal second, where nothing mattered except a fierce, overwhelming need to just let go.

She gasped as she neared it, rocked her hips against his touch, and as if he sensed her orgasm was close he stopped weaving his magic, his overpowering black magic, and rose. In a second he settled his big body on top of hers, bracing his upper body on his hands as he gazed down at her.

Her legs were still bent, her breasts crushed beneath her thighs, her knees tight to her shoulders. Sebastian's weight pinned her down, keeping her sex completely open and exposed to him.

Cleo writhed beneath him, seeking him, inviting him, for she knew that no one could fill this emptiness, this aching desire, except him. He moved his hips and paused, poised at her entrance where she could feel the tip of his cock lightly brush against her swollen pussy.

"Say it, Cleo," he said in a strained voice. The light in his eyes was dark and fierce and breathtaking. Their gazes locked for what seemed like an eternity.

"Fuck me, Sebastian," she finally breathed.

When he buried his cock inside her he cried out, the sound resembling that of a pained, dying animal. Cleo gasped, mesmerized by the feel of him so deeply embedded inside her, filling her, completing her. She clutched at his shoulders then spread her hands over the muscles of his back, pulling him closer.

"More, *more!*" she cried.

"You sexy little slut," he breathed, humping her with superhuman strength. "This is what you wanted wasn't it, you horny little bitch?"

"Yes, yes!" She rolled her head from side to side, desperate and straining for release. Whimpering, she slid her hands past his waist and clutched the hard, straining muscles of his buttocks, lifting her hips and urging him as deep inside her as he could manage.

"Look at me, Cleo."

She turned her face, her eyelids feeling heavy and hot as she gazed up at him. Sweat beaded his brow and his nostrils flared as he struggled for breath and stared down fiercely into her eyes. His jaw was tight with effort as he rammed inside her, veins straining against his neck.

"I want to watch when you come," he said heavily, his voice hot and broken with desire. All the while he kept thrusting and thrusting and thrusting inside her. "I want to see your pretty face when you come for me."

Her eyes widened as she reached the tip, the point, that painful second before release. "Now, Sebastian, *now!*" she cried.

With one last thrust he drove his cock straight home. Cleo clutched him tightly while he shuddered, his face contorted in ecstasy, and be it heaven or hell, she would follow him. Closing her eyes, she rubbed her sex against his hardness ever so slightly, and with that fleeting touch, exploded into a million pieces.

Fucking awesome.

No other words could describe her.

And now Sebastian didn't give a damn if he was being a real pussy for wanting to hold her. But he did, he wanted — *needed* — to hold her as much as he'd needed to fuck her. He gathered her into his arms and pressed her face into the crook of his neck. It was odd, the way the burning, fiery desire he'd harbored for years now felt like something else. Something fuzzy, warm. A feeling as alien to him as cuddling a woman after he'd screwed her. A feeling he'd thought was solely exclusive to wimps, gays and girls. That life-is-beautiful sort of crap. It was inside him now, and damn it, it felt good.

And Cleo, in his arms, felt even better.

His thoughts darkened when he remembered she would be going back to take care of those freaking old geezers tomorrow. She would fly back to Seattle, leaving him behind. But he couldn't let that affect him because tonight…tonight she was his. And for the life of him, he would be content with that.

For now.

It had been…

No. Cleo dared not even think it.

She should not think these things, for her brain was still clouded and hazy, not working properly—short-circuited. But try as she might, she couldn't stop the sting in her eyes and the feeling of having experienced something painfully beautiful. She sniffled softly when the tears came and prayed a silent prayer that he wouldn't notice. His hold tightened around her and he bent his head, pressing his brow to hers.

"What is this?" He took her chin between his thumb and forefinger and tilted her face upward. Cleo shyly met his gaze, acutely aware of her stinging red eyes and silently cursing herself for being so weak in front of him, so weak in front of a man who could break her as easily as a twig under his feet. "Why are you crying, Cleo?"

She bit her lip because frankly, she didn't know.

"Bas, are you making her cry *again*?" Luella asked, clearly concerned.

"Mind your own business," Sebastian snapped, glaring at her over his shoulder before he turned back to Cleo and tenderly rubbed his thumbs along her cheeks. "Don't cry, Cleo."

His concern tightened around her heart like a fist.

Staring into his eyes, the color of polished onyx, blazing with need and longing as he looked back at her, Cleo finally realized why she was so afraid of him—and why she wanted to cry. It wasn't him actually, but what she felt because of him. Hate. Pain. Want.

And so much love.

It was impossible to explain these strong, conflicting emotions with the same simplicity as she could explain something like a rainbow. Cleo couldn't understand them like she could understand the rightness of one plus one being two. She couldn't predict the outcome of an experience such as this like she could predict the outcome of a division or multiplication.

These feelings rioted, blended, mixed…and she could no more explain them than she could explain her own existence and meaning in this world. It scared her, the sheer intensity and power of her emotions, for she knew they had the power to lift her to the skies. Or destroy her completely.

"You regret this, don't you?" Sebastian asked gruffly.

"No, Sebastian, I don't."

He pressed his lips to hers softly, tenderly. "If I hurt you, I'm sorry."

"You didn't hurt me," she said, reaching to cup his hard, square jaw with her palms. She knew it the second she stared into his eyes, for she saw her heart right in them—she still loved him. Achingly. Deeply. And all these years, she always had. Yes, it hurt. He angered her, hurt her…and she still loved him.

"I'm sorry baby, for everything," he breathed as he pulled her to him and crushed his lips to hers.

She melted under his lips, under the pressure of his mouth urging hers to open for him. Her hands settled on the back of his neck while she met the thrusts of his tongue equally with those of her own.

She trembled in his arms before he pulled back, for the first time noting they were still naked. "Stay here," he whispered.

Rising, he left her for a minute and came back wearing his jeans and white cotton shirt, his jacket in his hand. He handed it to her. "Here, put this on," he said softly.

Cleo did so, slipping her arms into the long sleeves then pulling it closed tightly across her chest. The jacket smelled like him—leather, beer, man and cigarettes. She made it a priority to memorize his scent, drew in a deep breath and felt drugged, intoxicated by it.

Sebastian sat down beside her, wrapped an arm around her shoulders and pulled her to his side. He eyed her profile in silence. "We're going to have to talk about this, Cleo."

"Yes," Cleo agreed, nodding slowly.

He stared blindly out at the ocean for a moment and then back at her. "I just don't know what to say," he confessed.

She met his gaze and thought how beautiful his eyes were. How deep and dark. There was no trace of the strong, unyielding man she knew. His features were still strong, still masculine and powerful, but much less menacing to her now. "Let's not say anything then."

Tightening his hold around her shoulders he smiled, a slow cocky grin, so rare on his face yet so familiar to her—for she knew it by memory. "We'll figure it out."

"Hey, are we spinning the devil again?" Luella asked.

"Hell no, this is much better," Jason said. He was sprawled naked between Haley and Luella's nude, sweaty bodies. David sat beside them, half-dressed and pensive.

"Your June wedding is definitely off, David, I'm sorry to have to say," Luella said matter-of-factly. "Your bride will be really pissed when she finds out you fucked us."

"Just shut the hell up," he grumbled.

Haley laughed. "How convenient to consider the decency of your actions only *after* you came in my mouth, David."

"I didn't mean for it to happen." David glowered at the red plush toy, almost buried in the sand now. "Fucking spin devil."

Cleo turned to look at it, only its tail and chubby legs sticking out of the sand.

Yes, that mischievous spin devil. It had possessed them all. And yet the game and its red-tailed mascot had given Cleo something beautiful, something she could only be grateful for. Maybe the spin devil game had, in a way, helped her to admit all these feelings, wild and beautiful and scary, that Sebastian Russo stirred inside her—now and maybe always.

"I want you again," Sebastian whispered, his breath scorching her ear. "*God*, I want you so much."

Cleo closed her eyes at his words and felt yards of slow, dizzying swirls of desire travel along her body, spreading to touch every corner of her being as he slowly, hotly kissed her earlobe.

"I want you too," she whispered to the air, to the wind, the sky, the ocean—and him.

"Let's go inside."

As Sebastian lifted a shrieking, smiling Cleo into his arms and carried her toward the two-story house, the four remaining friends looked at each other in amusement.

"Think it's the love bug?" Haley asked, her eyes lively and glimmering.

"Yep," Jason said, nodding in approval.

David shook his head vehemently, scowling at the toy on the sand, already forgotten by everyone except him. "It's that damned spin devil."

Several slaps and smacks landed playfully on the back of David's head.

"Shut up, you old grump."

"Get over it, babe. Wedding's off."

"Is that what you're going to tell the blushing bride? 'The spin devil made me do it'?"

David watched the couple as they disappeared inside the house. If Sebastian and Cleo could make things work after years and years of heartache, then David could sure as hell make things right with his bride.

He smiled and nodded at his friends. "Hell yeah. It was the spin devil."

The End

SPIN IT AGAIN

෨

Trademarks Acknowledgement

સ૦

Chapter One

ও

David woke up with an empty bottle of beer in one hand and a blonde in the other. Groaning, he shifted on the bed and winced at the flash of pain in his gut and the sudden pounding in his head. Apparently oblivious to his pain, the blonde snuggled closer to him and he glowered down at her bleached hair. He couldn't even remember her name, although he could remember other things about last night with painstaking detail.

During their few minutes of sex, David had been vicious, desperate and cruel. Because more than sex, what he'd wanted — what he'd *needed* — was to kill someone.

His eyes darkened when he remembered the sordid, sorry events of last night.

He'd unexpectedly seen *her*, after one whole year of trying futilely to do so.

She'd been making out in a busy Manhattan nightclub. Someone else's hand had been crushing her breast through her shirt, his tongue tasting her mouth — the mouth of the woman David had planned to marry. The woman he loved. And she'd been making out. There. For everyone to see. For *David* to see. Making out. With a faceless, nameless asshole whose heart David wanted to rip out of his chest.

David had been drunk — which was nothing new. He'd spent little to no sober hours during the past year.

He'd never expected to see her, especially since she'd made it her life's mission to avoid him now. And yet there she was, Evie Mathews, *his* Evie Mathews — who should have been Evie Hawthorne by now — in a noisy nightclub featuring scantily clad ladies locked inside cages that hung from the ceiling. Huddled in a smoky, dark corner of the club, she'd been putting out for that bastard, in public, in a way she'd *never* put out for David.

Even from afar, he'd seen the exact moment her hand disappeared into the waistband of a well-worn pair of jeans and slowly began to fondle the man's dick underneath. She actually *touched* the bastard's filthy, sorry excuse for a cock—and David saw it all, saw the way she stroked that hideous thing with her dainty little hand. The same soft, fragile hand David had held and kissed as if it were something holy. The same hand that had rubbed David to climax hundreds of times. The same hand that, even while busily occupied touching someone else's privates, still managed to crush David's heart like a tin can. Watching that little hand move under those jeans, stroking up and down, made his own cock push hard against his underwear, desperate for her attentions…for her touch.

David remembered the evening too vividly…

Walking around in a dazed, drunken stupor, a blonde on each arm and a beer in each hand, David lazily alternated swigs from one to the other. It would have probably been an okay night if he hadn't seen her. Hell, it would have been an okay night if he didn't still *love* her. But he did see her, and he did love her, and he knew right then and there that he was going to fucking kill that son of a bitch sitting with a stiff cock beside her.

All hell broke loose when David lunged at him. Glasses crashed to the floor, the table toppled over and people screamed. All David knew was that someone had to die that night. It wasn't enough to sink his fists into the bastard's gut. Not enough to introduce his knuckles to his mean, fat jaw. Not enough to wrap his hands around the jerk's thick neck and squeeze with all his might.

The damned bastard was strong. And sober. Unlike David's sorry drunken state.

David took a punch to the stomach, one which made him fold over in pain. He jerked backward when a beefy fist landed on his jaw, blood spilling from his lips at the blow. David shook from the effort it took just to remain standing—and then his eyes met the man's gaze. Either David was killing that sorry motherfucker, or he'd be glad if the bastard killed *him* and put an early end to his sorry, miserable life.

Evie was shouting, her words barely getting past the roaring in his ears. She wasn't shouting the bastard's name, but *his* name. David's name. It echoed in his ears like a siren song as he slammed his fist into the bastard's nose, sending him tumbling backward. After readying his fists to deliver yet another blow, one that would hopefully kill the bastard, a pair of hands suddenly locked his arms behind his back, and David bucked wildly in an effort to release himself.

"Sir, I'm going to have to ask you to step outside," a deep voice said.

It was someone from the club's security, and as David's wild, wrecked gaze scanned the club, he noticed there were several more of them winding their way through the crowd, speaking into the tiny microphones on their collars as they approached.

"I'll escort my own fucking self out!" he thundered, yanking his arms free.

But before he did as he promised, he looked at Evie, standing there looking just amazing, her chest heaving rapidly, her face flushed, her blue eyes big and scared and beautiful.

He pointed a finger straight at her, his eyes narrowed, his nostrils flaring with each breath he took. "You're *mine*, do you hear me?" He slammed his palms to his chest. "You're fucking *mine*."

On his way out, he fell on the sidewalk outside the club, suddenly weakened by the sight of her. One of the blondes—the one who *didn't* run away scared shitless—wrapped her arms around him and helped him wobble across the lobby when they arrived at his building. Once in his apartment, she'd giggled sexily and brushed blood away from his lips so she could kiss him.

He remembered going crazy, tearing her clothes off, forcing her to her knees and sticking his cock into her mouth. Every single word he'd said then, he'd meant for someone else.

"Fucking bitch. You damned horny bitch. Did you want cock? Is that what you wanted, you hot, horny slut? Did you want his cock inside you?"

The blonde had thought it wise to shout a big, effusive "Yes!" to everything he said. Seriously, he could've killed her for that—he was so damned pissed. Just to let her know she was in serious danger, he growled a low, terrifying sound to rival that of every monster in any horror movie he'd ever seen. Still she didn't quite get it, and instead pouted her lips and looked up at him dreamily.

"Yes! I'm a slut. A big, fat, horny slut…punish me, punish me *now*!"

Did her speech serve to appease him? Hell no. Only having Evie there—twisting her hair like he twisted the blonde's, forcing her down on all fours and taking her like a bitch in heat—would serve to appease him. Maybe even making that bastard she was with watch while he did so.

The blonde had yelped and whimpered and begged for more even as he slapped her buttocks with his palms and rammed his cock into her ass without the slightest concern for her whatsoever. She clutched at her own tits, squeezed and pinched her nipples and even furiously pushed her butt back against his hips, as if his thrusts weren't harsh enough to suit her.

She had a nice, tight little ass. It molded around his cock like clay, making him grit his teeth from the effort it took just to push and keep on pushing into that tiny, pink puckered hole. Every erotic sound, the low and the loud, tore from her lips as he fucked her, punished her, made her regret touching that cock, made her regret wanting it. She wasn't some random blonde, she wasn't a stranger.

She was Evie. On all fours, screaming her head off, taking his cock deep inside her ass and shoving back for more. It was Evie squeezing her own tits, bending her head down and pulling up a breast to her lips so she could suck on her own nipple. It was Evie sliding a hand past her navel and cupping her pussy in her hand, slowly circling her clit with her finger before sticking it into the wet, gleaming folds of her cunt. And it was Evie letting him fuck her in the ass, letting him have his way with her, while she touched herself, licked herself, like the little bitch she was.

He cried out her name when he came, spilling into her ass, his voice sounding hoarse and pained. Then everything had become deathly still, the sound of his breathing suddenly magnified by the awkward silence in the room.

Only minutes afterward, David had felt so desolate that he buried himself beneath the bedsheets with his last bottle of beer and conveniently forgot about the blonde who'd graciously stood in for Evie—just as some poor girl always did.

Yet most of them didn't seem to mind. He'd fucked numerous ladies at the nearby strip club he'd been frequenting, where every night the manager—now his very good pal—unfailingly offered David the best seat in the house, just so he could sit, get drunk and watch the elegant, artistic display of tits and ass. The girls rode that pole pretty damn well, and they rode *him* even better, but he didn't know any of their names. To him, they were just bodies—cunts and tits and tongues—and there was only one name he whispered when he came, every damn time. One name he cried out in the midst of his drunken passion. His good chum the manager, knowing what a discriminating customer like David preferred by now, had already instructed the girls…

If David were to choose one of them for some serious adult fun, she'd have to do a little role-playing—and above all else, she'd *have* to pretend her name was Evie.

Only last week, David had brought home a pair of Asian twins—each calling herself Evie—and had gotten one hell of a decent blowjob. Their tongues had been pierced and they'd used the smooth gold pebbles to tease his cock mercilessly.

Lying on the bed and staring dazedly up at the ceiling, David had grabbed the twin kneeling between his thighs and shoved her face lower, down to his throbbing balls. The other twin was kneeling by his side, slowly milking his cock with her mouth. Purring deep in his throat and closing his eyes, he ran his hand down her spine, dipping a finger between her buttocks until he'd buried it in her ass.

"Do you like that, Evie?" he asked hoarsely, and she purred against his cock, making him shudder as she ran the warm gold ball around the tip of his shaft.

He fisted his hand in the other twin's hair, tightly pressing her face to his nuts while ordering her to suck harder. She not only sucked harder, but slid a finger into his ass while she did so, pumping it inside him while she scraped the metal stud around his sac.

David went wild, rocking his hips against one mouth while the other nibbled at his balls, sending his senses reeling. Then two fingers pummeled deep into his ass, tearing a groan from deep in his chest. It was then, shivering with sensations, when he'd ordered them to *dare* tell him to his face what a two-timing, cheating bastard he was. They'd obeyed with gusto, cursing him loudly, fervently, not even their charming accents detracting from the harshness of their words.

He hadn't anticipated that hearing both women call him less-than flattering names would really tick him off, so he'd grabbed their hair and yanked their heads back—*hard*. Cursing them right back for every low, coarse word they'd uttered. Cursing them for being such selfish, unforgiving bitches. He didn't know if they'd minded his roughness, but hell, he was paying for it and they'd let him.

Still mumbling curses under his breath, he'd pressed their faces back to his privates, ordering them to suck him and make him come. Between their moaning and mewling, they continued to blow him until he shattered and cried out that tormenting, beautiful name. Then they'd touched themselves, fondling their pussies as they sought their own climaxes. If they'd expected anything but a good tip afterward, they were sorely mistaken. At that point, they should have known he really *was* a lying, two-timing, mean and horny bastard, one who'd betrayed the woman he loved. What did they expect from someone like him?

Apparently, the blonde from last night had expected just that sort of treatment...and she'd damn well *loved* it.

After he'd brutally screwed her, she'd still thought it would be a good idea to get comfy and snuggle up beside him — as if David could possibly be chummy and cuddly while in his current state of mind.

In this hateful, diabolical, plain suicidal state of mind.

In his whole cursed life, he'd never thought he could hate someone as much as he hated himself *and* the sorry bastard who'd touched his girl.

But he especially hated Evie — for not loving him hard enough to forgive him.

Staring down at the blonde, an unwanted, disturbing reminder of yesterday, David shoved her away from him and rose from the bed, the move sending another jolt of pain to his stomach as he headed naked toward the bathroom. Bracing his hands on the sink, he stared at his own reflection in the mirror. The man he saw bore no resemblance to the man he'd once been.

David had been a happy man. A man who knew how to smile, who'd loved his job and who'd thought himself to be one of the precious few souls lucky enough to find true love in this lifetime. He'd found the love of his life, the one to spend his whole life with...and lost her.

The man in the mirror didn't look like David Hawthorne. He looked harsh, angry. He hadn't shaved in days. Thick strands of dark brown hair fell carelessly past his ears, testifying to his year-long rebellion against fashion and grooming. His skin was tanned, but dull and lifeless. His features were vicious and etched with pain, his jaw more pronounced now and clenched much too tightly for comfort. His sleek, dark eyebrows arched before angling downward, gifting his face with a permanent scowl. There was a death wish there, in the way his lips were set, in the steely glint in his dark brown eyes. He was crazy. A man gone mad.

He'd been fired from his high-stakes, high-paying job on Wall Street after he'd attacked his boss when he'd dared tease him about his broken engagement. His comment had not been the least bit frickin' funny, although apparently his boss had thought so. David had brusquely shoved him up against a wall, wanted to see if he thought *that* was funny, which he obviously hadn't.

When he'd been fired, David had remarkably felt—nothing.

Nothing.

His job meant nothing to him anymore. His whole life meant nothing. And it was no one's fault but *his*.

And maybe that damned spin devil's.

And Evie's. For not forgetting...not forgiving.

David curled his fingers around the ring that hung from his neck. He yanked on the chain, tearing the weak gold links open, and fisted his hand around it.

Gathering his courage, he spread his palm open to reveal the diamond solitaire ring. For a few precious months, it had been Evie's ring.

It was no one's ring now.

The diamond glinted mockingly at him and David gritted his teeth, the sight of it bringing fresh, searing pain anew. This time not to his ribs, nor to the cut at the side of his lips, but to his heart. His very soul.

He'd replayed that day a million times in his head already. Wondering if he'd said something differently, done something differently, she would have forgiven him.

How fucking fragile their love had turned out to be.

He'd once thought they were invincible. He'd thought that, with Evie beside him, he could take on the world.

One mistake. That's all it took. One fucking mistake and he'd lost everything.

It had been a windy day, the day he'd returned to New York from a weekend trip to Florida, where he'd met with his college buddies. He'd been too caught up with work during the last couple years to pay any attention to what was going on with their lives, and it had seemed like a fun idea to see them again. Sebastian, always the rebel. Jason, the best pal to get drunk with. Luella, with her loud voice and even louder opinions. Cleo, about the sweetest person at their college, and Haley, always fun and easygoing.

It had been the biggest mistake of his worthless, piece-of-shit life.

That, and having been way drunk by the time they'd indulged in a game called "spin devil" that Luella had suggested. They'd spun a plush red devil as if it were a bottle, and dared and taunted each other mercilessly. As the night progressed, the group got drunker and the dares got riskier. During his final dare, Sebastian couldn't pass up the opportunity to get Cleo naked, and pretty soon all his friends followed. Caught up in the moment, David ended up with his mouth buried in Luella's cunt while Haley sucked him off. Both women were his friends, and he'd never intended to fuck them, but things got wild. Crazy. As if the satiny little devil had robbed them completely of their senses.

David regretted every fucking minute of it.

The day he got back to New York he'd taken a cab straight home, where he and Evie had been living together for several months after he'd left his own apartment in the Upper West Side. The guilt on his shoulders weighed heavily and he couldn't stand the feeling of the burning black poison running through his veins, product of the sheer hate brewing inside him. He had to tell her, tell her now. Evie *knew* he loved her. She *knew* he loved her more than anything in the world. She would know it hadn't meant anything to him, nothing but a good time. She'd understand it had been nothing but a foolish, reckless moment. He had to tell her, and if she loved him, she had to forgive him.

When she opened the door, David felt like he'd been punched in the gut, the air wheezing out of his lungs with roaring speed. She looked so beautiful, her face glowing with excitement, her heart shining in her eyes as she gazed up at him, at the man she was engaged to marry, as if he were her hero.

Some fucking hero he'd turned out to be.

"Baby, you're home!" she said happily, flinging herself at him, wrapping her arms around his neck. His arms encircled her waist and he held her to him, held her closely.

"Evie."

It was all he could say. That word meant everything to him. It meant I love you, I missed you, I want you, I need you…and I'm sorry. I'm so sorry.

Inhaling the sweet scent of her shampoo, David closed his eyes and tightened his hold on her. She felt so small against him, so delicate. God help him, no matter what happened, he would *never* let go of her. He was crazy about her.

"Honey…you're squishing me. I can't breathe." Her voice was muffled by his chest as she struggled to free herself.

He pulled back and looked at her, his eyes insatiable as they roamed over her face. She was the most beautiful thing in the world to him. Her blue eyes danced with excitement, her small pouted lips forming a wide, sincere smile. Her skin was flawless, white and pure, sharply contrasting with the inky blackness of her hair, worn loose past her shoulders like a mass of heavy black silk. A light shade of pink tinted her cheeks, giving her skin a soft glow. She had the face of a doll, her features delicate and feminine, soft and rounded. To him, no Renoir, Botticelli or any other master ever created *anything* that could begin to compare to Evie's classic beauty. She was worthy of placing on an altar with candles all around her.

"I need to tell you something." He was barely able to speak when he took a step forward and closed the door behind him. His heart pounded harsh and loud against his rib cage. The way he felt, he could have carried the whole city on his shoulders and the load would have been lighter.

Her smile vanished completely at his words, and there was concern in her eyes as she cupped his face with one fragile little hand. "Did something happen?"

It was painful, to feel her skin against his, so soft and warm. Closing his eyes, he rubbed his jaw against it, savoring the feel of her touch, the gentleness of it. "You feel so good. I missed you so much," he said hoarsely.

"David." She sounded alarmed. "What's wrong?"

He opened his eyes and looked right into her breathtaking blue gaze. By the time he'd gathered enough courage to speak his stomach was already tied into a thick, tight knot.

"I had sex this weekend."

It was like watching a murder, like being witness to a war.

He saw the way the beautiful vivid light in her eyes completely, totally vanished. He saw the way her skin paled from rosy to ashen. He saw the way her features—always beautiful, always perfect—distorted with pain.

She retracted her hand from his face, not wanting to touch him now, but David felt frantic, grabbing her hand midway and pressing it back to his cheek.

"It didn't mean anything, Evie. I love *you*," he quickly said, squeezing the hand he held forcibly to his cheek. "Only you. Always."

She shook her head wildly, looking hurt and pained and confused. "No, no, no—don't say this!" She yanked her hand free from his and took a step backward, still shaking her head.

He stretched his arms out to her. "We were all drunk, playing games...and one thing led to another. I never meant for it to happen, but then Cleo and Bas were going at it and Haley dropped my pants—"

"Shut up! *Just shut up*! I don't want to hear it!" She clamped her palms over her ears, all the while shaking her head, her eyes shimmering with tears as she stared at him in disbelief. Her lips trembled and David suddenly felt his own eyes flood with tears.

What kind of a motherfucker was he to do this to her? What kind of a freakin' pathetic asshole would do this to the woman he *loved*?

"Evie, I love you!" he shouted in desperation. He reached for her and hauled her to his body, crushing her to him.

Stiff and unyielding, she pushed herself away with surprising force, immediately turning her back to him. "Don't touch me," she whimpered.

The sound of her breathing was louder and harsher than those itty-bitty words. But those words, no matter how softly spoken...oh, how they hurt. How they tore through his chest. They coiled around his heart like a snake, crushing it.

Ignoring the clenching pain that tore through his insides, he cupped her shoulders from behind. She cringed at his touch, visibly sickened by him.

"Please forgive me," he whispered in her ear, his hold on her shoulders tightening while he repeated those words like a chant. "Please, *please* forgive me."

And then he went crazy, because he knew he had to have her. He had to sink himself inside her, had to *know* she was still his, had to *know* if she still loved him, if she would forgive him this. This betrayal.

Frantically he nuzzled her earlobe, dipping his tongue into her ear as he slid his hands past her shoulders. He cupped her breasts and pressed her body back against his. "I want you. *God*, I need you," he whispered hotly. Every inch of his body shook with fear, with longing and desire.

She was rigid against him, and her lack of response scared him. It made him want to pour his soul out to her, made him want to find a way to make her melt, make her forgive him, make her his. Trailing a path of hot, urgent kisses down her neck, he squeezed one breast while he lowered a hand to cup her sex over her jeans.

"It wasn't like with you," he said desperately. "Nothing compares to you, Evie. *Please*, baby, please don't let this break us."

The sudden sound of her sobs wrecked him completely. They tore from somewhere deep, so very deep inside her—slicing him like a thousand knives driving into his flesh at once. Along with the clenching in his throat he felt his own tears then, spilling without notice, skidding slowly down his cheek and onto her shoulder. For the first time, he wondered how they would *ever* be able to make this thing, this pain, this cursed mistake go away.

"How could you?" she whispered shakily, not even turning to face him.

"*Please forgive me, Evie.*" He'd never uttered those words with so much passion, so much meaning, ever. His eyes stung as he fought to hold his tears back but just looking at her, looking at what he was doing to her, was enough to make him want to kill himself.

Feeling desperate, he whirled her around and kissed her, kissed her rough and hard, sinking his tongue into her mouth. She didn't pull away but she was frighteningly unresponsive, not kissing him like she used to, all eagerness and playfulness and love. She was still sobbing even as his tongue slowly stroked the soft, pliant cavern of her mouth. Tears continued to slide down his cheeks as well, but that wouldn't stop him from kissing her. He pressed his lips to hers harder, trying to deepen the kiss. He knew that just one night, one night of loving Evie, and everything would be all right, everything would be like it used to be.

It just wasn't going to happen.

She pulled away from him then, slowly, not angrily like he'd expected, but so damned hurt. "Here. I don't want this," she said, placing something in his palm, his fingers reflexively closing on it. She kept her face lowered, as if she couldn't stand looking at him, and her voice trembled when she spoke. "I'll let the judge know."

David glanced down at his hand, slowly uncurling his fingers so he could stare down at the object—her ring. The one he'd given her three months ago tied to the stem of a single red rose. At the mere sight of it, he knew—this was what it felt like to fall into the deepest, darkest pits of hell.

Even now, one year later, David felt that familiar knot in his throat, that clenching in his gut and the excruciating pain in his heart.

Hell.

He'd been living there for a whole year, a fucking resident, maybe almost president by now. He'd called her a million times, sent her trucks of flowers, faxes, emails. He'd tried cajoling, begging, explaining. His calls, emails and intentions went unanswered, and his flowers were unfailingly returned.

The thought that Evie might never forgive him hadn't occurred to him until he got a call from her eldest brother, Gregory, a man whom David had done business with and had always admired and respected.

"Haven't you've hurt my sister enough, David?" he'd demanded. "She's trying to get on with her life, and if you have the slightest amount of decency you should lay off, for God's sake. Stop following her, stop calling and just leave her the hell alone. She *doesn't* want to see you."

"I love her, Gregory!" David had shouted, but Gregory had already hung up.

A half-hour later, David had found himself locked in the stinking bathroom stall of a nearby establishment, screwing the brains out of a curvy waitress in a striped uniform. She'd smiled at him three times while he'd sat at the restaurant-bar, so he figured she was practically begging for it. He followed her to the restroom, covered her mouth with his and pumped inside her so hard and fast that all the woman could do was hold on tight.

He'd ripped the top of her uniform open and when her tits spilled out, sucked and bit on them fiercely. She clutched his hair and the one time she spoke called him "pretty boy". He didn't care. He'd actually called her something worse *plenty* of times.

When they were finished, she'd claimed to be a little "bewildered" but still offered her phone number, acting all charming and giggly, despite his deadly frown. Before she tumbled all over herself to get a pen, he simply lifted a hand to halt her and said, "Don't bother."

Leave her alone.

The words haunted him every day, every second, no matter if he was drunk or screwing someone—or, at the way things were heading, screwing *something*. Anything.

Anything to forget. Anything to forget *her*…and leave her the hell alone.

So David had left her alone, hoping if he gave her time to heal she would forgive him. If he demonstrated that he *did* have a shred of decency, enough of it to give her space and time to think, she would forgive him. He kept thinking if she loved him, she *should* forgive him. Then he thought one way or another, she *had* to forgive him.

He'd sunk himself further into hell as he waited for her, as he drank to forget, fucked to forget, while every day that went by effectively managed to kill another little bit of his hope.

Hope.

He had none of it now, not after seeing her last night, with that bastard.

David glanced at himself in the mirror again and narrowed his eyes. He had to do something. He couldn't live like this, not without her, and not while knowing she was traipsing all over the city, putting out for some cheap bastard. She was *his*, damn her! He loved her, wanted her, *needed* her, and if he didn't have her, he knew he'd die from this. This sickness, this hatred of himself, this pain of loving her.

Damn her for not forgiving him!

Damn her for making out with that motherfucker, that horny little bitch!

He conveniently forgot about the dozens of Evie impersonators he'd screwed ten ways to Sunday since the beginning of his downward spiral, because those women didn't matter. He did what he did out of depression and loss and unbearable pain.

Not to mention, he already knew he was worthless piece of scum.

But Evie was *not*. David had wanted to wring her neck right there in the club and stick his hand into her pants, see if she was wet for that ugly asshole, just so he could have proof enough to go ahead and kill him.

With renewed vigor and determination, he stormed into the bedroom and pulled out a shoebox from under the bed, yanking off the top. Pulling out the red stuffed toy, the damned spin devil, he glared down at its beady black eyes and squeezed the little shit with his hands as if he could drain the life out of it. "You're not screwing up my life, you stinking little prick," he hissed.

There were rustling sounds coming from the bed, and a soft, female "Huh?"

He whipped his gaze up to the intruder, his face a mask of rage. "You know where the door is."

Chapter Two

෨

You're mine.

Sitting in a crowded spot on the metro as she rode home from work, Evie felt her heart constrict while David's words played in her head over and over again.

Sadly, Evie couldn't help but agree—despite how painful the truth was to her.

You're mine.

You're fucking mine.

She clutched her purse to her chest, suddenly needing to hold on to something while she tried futilely to block his words out of her head.

This past year, all she'd been focused on was surviving. Surviving and living—without him. She'd held on to that hate, that blissful hate, the only thing that had kept her heart beating for the past year. Hating him. Cursing him. Damning him.

She took it one day at a time, one measly day at a time, never knowing for sure if she'd be able to get through each without bursting into tears or doing something worse. She felt like a crazy person—fine one moment and struck by a raging, blinding pain the next.

Once, while she'd strolled down the streets of Manhattan with her friend Fiona, she'd caught sight of a lone red rose, like the one David had tied her engagement ring to, sticking out of a newspaper stand. Evie had made some surprisingly sick noises as she yanked it out and destroyed it completely, cutting herself with a thorn in the process. Afterward, feeling a little embarrassed while eyeing the remains of the flower scattered over the sidewalk, she'd dutifully paid for it.

Evie's problem wasn't that rose. It was everything, because David was everywhere.

She'd thrown away her bedsheets because it had been impossible to wash out his smell. His closet space was still achingly empty in their bedroom, and she couldn't seem to buy clothes fast enough to fill the void. He was in every stock news channel she clicked by on TV, in every Meat Loaf song, in every takeout Chinese box and every Twix chocolate bar. His kisses were there in every single kiss she saw, and the way he'd loved her shone in every drawing of a heart, every smile, every couple she saw walking by.

Three years were hard to forget for anyone, but to Evie it hadn't been just three years—it had been her future too, for she'd dreamed it perfectly, and every piece of it had included *him*.

It had taken a single night in Florida, a couple of drinks and two naked women to deny her heart of every dream it had nurtured, every hope, every longing. And while her dreams had vanished, every memory of him had grown...every memory from the very first moment she'd met him.

He'd been dining with one of his clients at a fancy Manhattan restaurant, while Evie had been dining with friends. She'd sat at a nearby table and he didn't take his eyes off her the whole evening. At the dark intensity of his gaze, Evie had felt as if a million butterflies had exploded from their cocoons right inside her stomach. He'd left the restaurant before she and her friends did, and when Fiona ordered the check, the waiter said it had been taken care of by "the gentleman with the black tie".

Her friends, in all their excitement, had immediately declared themselves in love with him. When they strode out onto the sidewalk Evie saw him, leaning against a car, looking so incredibly gorgeous. He straightened when he saw her, a slow smile spreading his lips. She knew then, as certain as she felt the melting in her bones, that he'd been waiting for her.

He walked her home that evening, and for the first time in her life Evie could finally put a face to the man of her dreams. David's face. Because she knew, without a doubt, that it was him.

She remembered the first "I love you" only a few months after they'd met, when he'd taken a long flight to Spain where he was scheduled to close a deal with one of his clients. Before he'd left, they made hot, reckless love in his apartment and he gently promised to be back in three days. On the third morning Evie woke up to the phone ringing, and when she answered, he'd been calling her from the plane on his way back to Manhattan.

"Did I wake you?" he'd asked, the sound of the jet engines humming softly in the background.

She'd sat up on the bed and swallowed several times, trying to sound like she'd been awake. "No. Yes…" Then she'd laughed, realizing she'd blown it.

"I'm in love with you, Evie," he'd said, his voice solemn and so dear to her.

Evie had known it for some time, for he'd shown her in a million ways. In the way he looked at her, the way he shielded her from the rain, the way he made love to her and the way his voice changed when he said her name. But hearing him say the words, especially when she was so madly in love with him herself, had been about the closest thing to heaven she'd ever experienced.

That and, of course, the day he'd proposed.

He'd just moved in with her and they'd had a silly fight over his dressing habits. Evie found it really annoying that he could be so organized at work and so damned sloppy at home. She was always picking up after him and she'd told him repeatedly that she was *not* his personal maid. That day, she swore to herself she wouldn't touch his things. Let him see if he appreciated living like a pig when he realized if *he* didn't pick his shit up, then nobody else would either.

When she got home from work he was already there, his feet propped up on the coffee table as he calmly flipped through a magazine. Evie still wasn't talking to him, and though she noticed a long-stemmed rose lying on the floor, she made a point not to pick it up.

When she walked past it several times, he finally dropped the magazine and looked up at her, clearly annoyed. "Aren't you going to pick that up?" he'd angrily asked.

"No," Evie said stubbornly, crossing her arms across her chest.

"Pick it up, Evie," he gritted out.

"I said *no*. I'm not your maid."

"Dammit." He stormed across the living room and grabbed it. "Here," he said, thrusting the flower toward her. "You were *supposed* to pick it up."

"Ha, you wish! I told you, David, *I'm not your maid*!"

He lifted the rose to her eye level and she saw something glinting from the stem. "But will you be my wife, Evie?"

That night, he'd made sweet, lazy love to her. He'd spoken soft, sweet words in her ear, promised he would love her, always love her, forever.

He'd lied.

And how it hurt to be mocked by her memories, to wonder if she'd made them all up, for the David she knew would have *never* done something like this to her. Every second of every day he was in her heart, in her mind, and it was worse than any other torture she could imagine.

Sometimes she would remember him smiling and playful, like he'd always been. More times than she wished, she remembered him as he'd been that afternoon, that horrible afternoon when they'd broken up, when he'd looked haggard and pained and haunted.

During the past year, the past horrible, nightmare of a year, Evie had experienced a tornado of emotions—hate, need, want and longing. And always this sick, distressing, painful love. She'd rather hate him. Hate was less cruel to her soul.

He'd been unfaithful…

Evie had been experiencing abundant, vivid nightmares about him, about him with those women, fucking and yelling and groaning while Evie had been at their apartment, watching a romantic comedy—thinking of him and wistfully planning their upcoming wedding. She'd called his hotel room every half-hour or so that night, needing to hear his voice before she went to sleep. She should have known there was something wrong when he didn't call her. She should have known there was something wrong with *her*.

Evie had been experiencing her share of sick, poisoning thoughts, some suggesting that maybe this had all been her fault. More times than not they made her wonder what in the world had been wrong with her.

Had she been no fun in bed? Had she been too boring, too shy? She remembered plenty of times when David had wanted to deviate, when he'd gotten a devilish glint in his eye and proposed something naughty. Evie would laugh and dismiss his comments, convinced he was teasing—surely he didn't mean it when he said he wanted to watch her masturbate while she watched porn on TV. Did he?

But now she feared she should have perhaps listened, been less afraid, less inhibited. Maybe if she'd been more open this never would have happened.

Did all women who had unfaithful partners feel this way? Was it fair that she should think she was partly to blame?

She wished she hadn't encouraged him to take that trip to Florida. He should have stayed in New York with *her*—where he belonged. But David had always glowed whenever he talked about his college friends and he'd been so tired from work, while Evie had been so busy with the wedding preparations. She thought it would be good for him. A well-deserved vacation.

The night before he left he'd made love to her against the wall, with his jeans at his ankles and his hips pushing forward and back, forward and back as he slid his cock—that lovely, perfect specimen—inside her. She'd wrapped her ankles around his waist and moaned feverishly while she begged and whimpered, "Yes, oooh yes, baby, more, more…"

"You make me so hot," he'd whispered while dragging his lips all over her face, kissing every inch of it. "So hot, so crazy."

It had been the last time Evie had had sex. The last time she'd held David in her arms, felt him inside her. David. *Her* David. Just to think of his cock inside another woman, while Evie waited for him at home…

It was every woman's nightmare…and it had happened to *her*.

She'd cried and cried and cried some more. Oceans of tears. Not even the girl-talk therapy her friends offered helped alleviate her pain. She'd had dozens of discussions with her closest friends, the sole topic being whether Evie had brought this on herself. Nobody thought she had—except Evie.

Throughout the last year and with a vengeance to rival a massive world war, Evie had dated every available man within her vicinity. Her friends had been shocked—this was very unlike her—including Fiona who, over coffee, had asked, "What are you trying to prove, going out with all these guys?"

"Nothing, I just don't feel like staying cooped up in my apartment," Evie had said as casually as she could manage.

Fiona had looked at her with pity as she'd squeezed Evie's hand in hers. "Evie, if David screwed up, he screwed up. It had nothing to do with you."

Deep down, Evie didn't believe that. If he loved her like she'd once *thought* he did, why did he screw around on her?

Why would he look for loving somewhere else, if not for the fact that he wasn't satisfied with Evie?

It *must* have had something to do with her.

Last night, when she'd been futilely trying to prove to herself that she could be just as hot, just as adventurous as the next woman, fondling a stranger that had flirted with her at the club, she'd never expected David would storm in out of the blue—tumbling drunk, with two bombshells following him like poodles.

Looking at him, she'd sought that hate, that comforting red-hot feeling, and found she couldn't hold on to it, couldn't even summon it. Just a look at those steely brown eyes and all she'd felt was pain, fresh and burning and new. Just standing there, so near, he'd torn her scar open. Evie could almost hear it as it tore, could almost hear the blood gushing inside her. Burning. Poisoning her insides with more pain, more love, more hate.

You're mine.

You're fucking mine.

He could have taken her then and there, made love to her in that club full of people, mad, drunken, crazy love, and Evie wouldn't have protested. A wild, desperate urge to feel him, an urge to know he still loved her, wanted her, wanted her more than those women, clenched tightly inside her womb. Her sex had flooded with need, an aching, painful need for him. Only him. Evie wanted no one else.

When he'd left, aided by one of the blondes—whose hair Evie had wanted to pull out by the roots—she'd felt desperate.

For a crazy moment, the shortest of seconds, she'd wanted to run after him and beg him to come back to her, beg him to love her like he used to, to make love to her and take her to heaven and make this horrible, wretched pain go away.

The next minute, Evie felt sick. *Really* sick. She'd felt dizzy and out of breath and she had to rush to the ladies' room to vomit.

She stayed there for the rest of the evening.

* * * * *

You're mine.

It was still running through Evie's head when she reached her apartment. She shoved the door open and pushed it closed as she strode inside. Then she halted, suddenly confused when she didn't hear it slam shut behind her. Whirling on her heel, her breath caught in her throat.

There he was, standing in the threshold.

All six feet, two inches of him, every one of them soiled and sweaty. He looked like a crazed, deranged madman just escaped from the institution. His clothes were rumpled, his dark brown hair in complete disarray, his face set firmly into vicious, uncompromising lines and his sleek brown eyebrows, a shade darker than his eyes, joined in a fierce scowl above his nose. With mock flair, he dropped a suitcase on the floor and slammed the door shut behind him.

"Honey, I'm home." His voice was rough, dry and deadly.

Evie couldn't think, couldn't breathe and could barely keep her knees from folding. There was only one thing she knew — this man, this animal, was *not* here to beg.

Out of some natural survival instinct, Evie took a step backward when he took a step toward her, lifting a red object in the air for her to see.

"Tail, you give me a second chance." He paused, narrowing his eyes. "Pitchfork, you give me a second chance."

He set the object on the floor and spun it and for a moment she stood there, dazed, watching what appeared to be a stuffed little devil twirl around madly on the floor. When it stopped, the pitchfork was pointing in her direction.

Breathless, she lifted her gaze to his.

"Pitchfork," he said flatly, lifting his brows. "Guess what? I get a second chance."

Closing the distance between them, he grabbed her shoulders and yanked her to him. Gasping, she folded her arms between them, shielding herself from ending up completely smashed against his chest.

As she stared up at him, she knew she should be a little afraid. She'd *never* seen him like this. There was a savage, lost look in his eyes and a frightening, harsh sound to his breathing that didn't bode well for her. Yet instead of fear, what she felt was pain. Pain and a swift, hot, overwhelming fury. When she spoke, her whole body shook with the need for violence and her voice was but a low hiss. "In. Your. Dreams. You lying, cheating *bastard*!"

Growling, he curled his fingers around her arms and squeezed so hard he almost cut off her blood supply. "I'm *not* in the mood for games."

Although her insides quivered at the deadly tone in his voice, she held her ground against him. "I'm not the one with the toy," she spat back, trying futilely to jerk free from his hold.

He narrowed his eyes into thin, glimmering dark slits. "*Damn you*," he said, his voice filled with venom. "Damn you, Evie! I've given you time to calm down and think things through. I'm going fucking crazy and I want a fucking chance!"

"That's too damned bad, because you're not getting one!" she yelled, this time successfully tearing away from his hold and taking a step backward, all heated up now. "I can't believe you even have the balls to come here and *demand* I give you a second chance, as if you even deserve it after the way you betrayed me, lied to me and screwed around on me the first chance you got!"

"I'm sorry. *I fucked up*!" he yelled back.

"No, you fucked someone wh wasn't me!" she shouted, sinking her nails into her palms to keep from breaking something. "What? I wasn't hot enough for you? I couldn't satisfy your precious little fantasies? Was plain Evie just too damned boring for you?"

"Oh, you satisfied me all right," he said, lowering his voice and taking a step forward.

She took another step backward and inwardly cursed the dead end when she bumped against the back of the living room sofa.

"Believe me, Evie, you more than satisfied me. What about *you*—did that fat bastard satisfy you? Did he screw you like I do? Did he make you moan and beg and come like I do?"

She narrowed her eyes as he approached, secretly and strangely excited at the crudeness of his words. "If he did, you'd be the last person to know."

He growled, baring his teeth, startling white against his tanned skin. "Well that's a shame, because I'm in the mood for spilling some juicy details myself, and I'll just bet you'd love to hear." He swiftly unbuttoned, unzipped and thrust his jeans to the floor, his cock popping out of his underwear when he pushed them downward.

His face was a mask of raw, vicious rage when he inched it toward hers. "I sucked Cleo's tits," he said viciously, sliding his hands beneath her top and cupping her breasts over her bra, squeezing them hard. "They tasted damned fucking good." Pulling down the flimsy material of her bra, he flattened his thumbs over the straining points of her nipples, pushing on them. "Almost as good as yours." She whimpered when he grabbed those little crests and pinched them hard. "Then I got to watch while Jason put his dick between those huge tits and humped and humped until he came all over them."

Evie couldn't believe he was telling her this, couldn't believe he could be this cruel—but then she'd already seen how badly he could hurt her. Her voice when she spoke was only a breathless whisper but the words stemmed from the bottom of her soul. "You bastard."

"Come again?"

She cried in outrage when he suddenly tore her shirt open, growling low and deep in his throat when he caught sight of her flesh. "Yes, I'm one sick bastard...but wait...there's more," he said cruelly while he roughly removed her shirt and bra, throwing both behind him.

"David...stop."

He fully ignored her, his attention solely focused on her newly bared breasts, his eyes turning dark and livid with desire. "All that time, all I wanted was to get my butt back home and do that very same thing with *your* tits. Rub my cock between them, squeeze and push them hard...just like a bitch like *you* should like it."

She yelped from the shock when he bent down and circled a nipple with his tongue, soaking it wet. Then his mouth latched onto it and sucked hard, as if he could drink from her. Evie swayed, suddenly discovering she had no more strength to stay upright. He caught her, his arms firm around her waist while he sucked her nipple and sent hot, tingling vibrations down to her sex. "Don't," she said breathlessly. "Don't touch me..."

He growled his denial and took her other nipple, first nibbling the hard little point with his lips and then drawing it into his mouth completely, making low suckling noises when he did so. Weakened by the spasms of heat quivering in her body, Evie clutched his hair, trying halfheartedly to pull him away from her breasts. It was no use, for now he'd gone lower, his tongue slicking a wet path to her navel while his hands easily worked on the buttons of her pants.

"Don't," she breathed again. Lifting his face to hers with startling speed, he locked his lips to hers, silencing her protests.

Evie knew she shouldn't give in, knew there was a reason she should hate him, but she felt so needy and so feverish for his touch that she found herself wrapping her arms around his neck and kissing him back, unthinkingly allowing mad, free rein to her desires. Dear God. *No one* kissed her like he did. No one tasted like him. No one felt so strong, so right for her. Her body melded to his, her soft womanly spots easing magically against his hard ones. The head of his cock, so strong, so hard, brushed against her bare stomach, and she felt dampness on its tip as it rubbed against her skin.

He had no mercy. His tongue pillaged her mouth, thrusting inside hers with fast, furious strokes, letting her know in a very efficient way that he intended to claim her. Conquer her. Command her. His moves as he scraped his cock against her belly weren't gentle. They were rough and fast and they drove her mad, making her burn with the desire to open her legs and welcome him deep into her being.

This was not the usual tender and teasing David she knew. This was an animal, a beast of a man who was hurting and desperate and crazed. And she was equally hurt, equally desperate and crazed. For him. David. The man she'd wished to marry. Owner of her heart, her body, her soul.

He dropped her pants and thong to her ankles and pulled away from her, breathing harshly. "On the couch," he said darkly, pushing her around the sofa and brusquely shoving her until she sat. She bounced on the seat, slouching with her ass barely on the edge. Suddenly damning herself for not thinking coherently, because she shouldn't succumb so easily. She shouldn't still want him, love him, need him—not after what he'd done.

She shivered when he straddled her, bracketing her hips with his knees. Her eyes settled on his cock, throbbing and hard and long, slowly inching its way toward her breasts. His eyes were lethal, not showing an ounce of concern but instead glowing with a steely hardness.

"*This,*" he said fiercely, pressing her breasts together while he thrust his cock between them. "This is what I wanted to do to you as soon as I got back." He closed his eyes and rocked his hips, slowly easing his cock between her breasts. Her sex flooded with wanton juices as she watched his face, that strong, chiseled face, tighten with desire as he rubbed his dick against her flesh.

"Is this turning you on?" he asked coarsely, pushing her breasts tighter to his cock.

Evie made a low, needy sound in her throat, thinking she could die from wanting him.

"Want to hear more? I'm sure you're just *loving* it." He smiled down at her, a cold, cruel smile. "After Jason came all over Cleo's tits, Sebastian started screwing her and Haley dropped my pants to *suck my cock*," he said.

And suddenly she knew…

The hate in his voice wasn't directed at her. The hate, so strong now…was directed at himself.

Grabbing her by the hair, he held her still while he shifted his body and slid his cock past her quivering lips and into her mouth. "And you know what? She sucked and sucked and sucked, and when I came, she drank *all* my fucking cum."

Hate, jealousy, love and desire—it was all inside her, making her shiver, making her want. There were torrents of feelings, wild and explosive and potent and ugly. She should have pulled away at his harsh, hurting words. Words meant to hurt her, meant to tear her apart. Instead, Evie wanted nothing but to claim him, nothing but to show that Haley bitch that he was *her* man. His cock was *Evie's,* and she stroked it hungrily with her tongue as it dipped into her mouth, intent on showing David that she could do better than Haley, better than Cleo. Better than anyone.

He groaned when Evie tilted her head and drew his penis deeper into her mouth, wishing to immerse it completely, taking in as much of it as she could. She grazed her fingers over the delicate hairs on his scrotum while she continued to suck on his cock, shuddering in need when she heard the way his breath rushed out of him, hot and haggard and furious. Pulling back slightly, she ran her tongue along the head, tracing the deep pink folds before drawing only the tip into her mouth. He watched her, his eyes vicious and hot as he hungrily witnessed the way she sucked him.

"And while I pushed my cock into her mouth," he continued harshly, "I told her 'suck it, suck my cock, you starved little bitch'. And she was hot for it, couldn't get enough of it."

That fucking cum-eating bitch! Evie thought furiously.

She felt like hurting someone.

"And while she sucked and sucked my cock, Jason fucked her in the *ass*."

Evie wanted to die. Every emotion inside her felt so strong, so overpowering. And between all the hate, between all the love, was a red-hot, blazing desire and an insatiable hunger…for him.

Curling her hand around the base of his dick and stroking upward, she bent her head and lightly tugged the tender skin on his balls, first nipping it with her lips then gently pulling with her teeth. He groaned, throwing his head back and emitting a low, rumbling sound of anguish that reverberated in her ears and triggered threads of sensation up to whip and flutter inside her.

While she continued to gently tease the soft, heavy sac of his balls with her mouth, she eased one hand around his hip and cupped his buttock. Sinking her nails in, she pulled him closer so she could better suck on him and show him how good she was, show him what he missed by not marrying her, not marrying the Queen of Head, for giving his cock to someone who didn't know how to savor it like she did. She wanted to punish him, teach him she could be wild and sexy too. She could be just as good — better — than those two women combined.

"And you know what, *sweetheart*? You know what I was doing while Haley sucked my cock and Jason screwed her in the ass? All that time I ate and ate and *ate* Luella's cunt," he said, suddenly pulling away and dropping to his knees on the floor before her. "If you give me some now I'll show you just what I did to make her moan, make her come in my mouth."

Before she could protest, before her heart could shatter and her soul could die a sudden, brutal death by words, he'd forced her legs apart and shoved his wide chest between her knees.

Evie had shaved. She'd wanted to think she was sexy, wanted to think she would be having sex with some stranger soon. She'd wanted to prove to herself she was hot and desirable, and that David *hadn't* screwed around because she lacked something.

"God," he whispered, his tone rendering even more reverence to the word.

He stared at the glistening folds of her sex for a full minute, his eyes dark and filled with lust.

"So wet, so pink and smooth," he whispered, speaking directly to her pussy and not even meeting Evie's heavy-lidded, heated gaze.

He placed two fingers on her labia and pulled them open before sinking his head between her legs and slipping his tongue through her parted folds. Evie arched back, a moan tearing from her chest. Then his hands cupped her buttocks and lifted her so he could gain better access, and she thought she would die from sheer pleasure when his tongue began to spear inside her.

"No one could ever taste like you, Evie. No one," he muttered against her sex before slowly sliding his tongue upward to stroke her clit. Her nipples tingled when he sucked her clit with his full lips, and Evie rocked her hips against his face and cupped her breasts wantonly, rubbing and pinching her aching nipples. She was burning, shivering with heat, already a breath away from orgasm while he sucked her so slowly, with a lack of haste, an expertise that drove her to the brink of madness.

She spread her hands on the back of his head and pushed his face farther into her pussy while she arched her hips to meet him. "David," she breathed.

Splaying a hand on her buttocks and sliding the other toward the dip between them, he slid a roaming finger into her ass while he kept on sucking her.

She cried out at the sudden invasion, her eyes jerking wide open as she stared blindly up at the ceiling. "*Oh God!*" she breathed. His finger sank deep into her ass just as she felt his teeth lightly pull at her clit. She yelped both in pain and pleasure.

"*David,*" she gasped in desperation.

He pulled back, his chest heaving as he slowly rose to his complete height. He gazed down at her, a muscle clenching in his jaw, his eyes dark and hard and unholy.

"Now I want to know who's fucked *you*. And I want names."

Chapter Three

ร

When he saw how she shivered under his stare, it took all his effort to hold back the sudden impulse to kiss her, to hold her and comfort her. He wouldn't be tender—frankly, he *couldn't*—not when he was furious, not when he was mad-crazy jealous. Not before she told him if that damned bastard had buried himself inside her.

She was *his*. His Evie, sitting there breathless and shivering on the sofa, her porcelain white skin glowing with sweat. Her lips were moist and swollen and her eyes shone with lust—lust for David and no one else. But David had to know—he couldn't stand thinking someone had touched her, jacked her. Not while he'd been waiting for her forgiveness, drunk and desperate and screwing every cunt in the city just to make sure he wasn't dead.

Evie took her precious time replying and David was sure it was on purpose. She was torturing him, punishing him for what he'd done to her.

"No one," she finally said, shaking her head, locks of dark black hair falling over her shoulders.

"Bullshit!" He clenched his fists at his sides. "You were almost screwing a guy right before my eyes last night."

She straightened her spine, her face heating to a bright red as she lifted her chin up haughtily. "So it's okay for *you* to fuck two women while we were engaged but I can't fuck anyone now that you're *nothing* to me, is that it, David?"

Damn her. Those women meant nothing to him, how many fucking times did he need to tell her? He fucked up! He sank his hands into her hair and rubbed his fingers against her scalp. "You're mine," he gritted out. "Don't you ever forget that, Evie. *Ever.*"

"I'm nothing to you," she spat back, a burning spark igniting her eyes. "If I'd meant so much to you you'd never have done this to me!"

A low, sick sound tore from his chest when he grabbed her arms and pulled her to her feet. He crushed his lips to hers and kissed her hard—hard and savage. He poured every beating of his heart, every aching inch of his hot, sweaty body into that kiss, even though he was mad fucking jealous and wanted—*needed*—to know who had dared touch her while he'd been dreaming, suffering, begging for her forgiveness.

His kiss should tell her, once and for all, that he loved her more than anything in this world. And he was *not* giving her up. Not to some asshole, not to anyone. He'd barely been able to keep on living knowing how much he'd hurt her, and he'd barely been able to cope with the sheer desperation he felt in not knowing what the hell he could do to turn things back to the way they were.

"Tell me," he demanded when he pulled away. "Did he fuck you?"

She merely stared at him, her eyes sparkling with rebellion, and when she pursed her lips David began to shake with a hot, blinding rage as he realized she didn't plan to tell him.

"You little slut." Grabbing a fistful of her hair, he ignored her soft little whimpers as he arranged her body over the sofa until her arms draped over the back and her ass was in the air, completely exposed to him. Possessively, he spread a hand over her bare rump and scraped his thumb over the sensitive, lustrous white skin.

"You won't be kissing anyone again, you won't be touching anyone again and you certainly won't be *fucking* anyone again except *me*, you got that, Evie?" he said, slapping one buttock harshly. She jerked from the impact, her answer only a soft, painful yelp.

"Answer me."

She was silent, deathly still. Furious, he slid the tip of his cock down her buttocks, between the generous mounds of her flesh. "Answer me."

He could hear her fast, loud breathing, could feel her wetness seeping like cream from her pussy, but still no answer.

"Answer me, Evie!"

"Yes."

His heart expanded in his chest at that word, only a whisper but enough to make him shake with the aching sweetness of victory. Roughly, he cupped her waist and readied himself behind her. "You're mine, Evie. Your heart. Your soul. Your body. Your pussy. Your ass. It's *all* mine."

He groaned when the tip of his cock found her entrance, slick and open for him, and with one swift thrust he rammed inside. They both cried out, their cries harsh and deep and animal and reverberating in the room so loudly that more than one neighbor must have paused to listen.

Let them hear. Let them *all* hear.

He began to move inside her, his eyes settling on the white, sweaty skin of her back and the rising little points of her spine. His thrusts weren't lazy or meant to please her. They were meant to let her know he was a man she shouldn't underestimate, meant to let her know she was his. *No one* would touch her while David still lived.

Yet as he sank himself balls-deep inside her, he painfully realized it wasn't enough. Demanding she be his, brutally claiming her body, was not enough. There was something he needed, something he couldn't demand she give him, something she had to give to him freely and honestly and completely.

He slowed his rhythm and bent forward, his chest pressing against her back and his face framed by the crook of her neck.

"Evie," he whispered hotly, brokenly, not wanting this anger anymore, wanting love, only love. And forgiveness. "Baby, I love you," he whispered, planting a hot, wet kiss on her ear. "I don't want to hurt us any more..."

She shivered beneath him and he wrapped his arms around her waist, the move making his cock slide just a bit farther inside her. That sensual movement proved to be excruciatingly painful to him and he felt a stinging, burning sensation in the pit of his being.

"Baby," he whispered hoarsely. "Please...please find it in your heart to forgive me. Maybe if you forgive me, I'll be able to forgive myself..."

Her cunt clenched around his cock as he spoke, as if his words affected every muscle in her tender, pliant body. Deathly still, he waited for her answer, his dick buried deep inside her, pulsing, throbbing. Her sex muscles instinctively quivered and massaged his cock, tightening and pulling him in.

She turned her face to look at him and he saw the tears shining in her eyes, on the verge of spilling. "You said you'd never hurt me."

"I'm sorry."

"You said you'd always love me."

"I do. Baby, I do—I love you more than anything."

"You made me want to *die*!"

Gently, he brushed his chin against the curve of her shoulder then kissed it softly, with a tenderness exclusive to that which was most precious to him. "I swear I'd kill myself before I hurt you again."

She made a little sound of pain in her throat and he tightened his hold around her waist. "I've been in hell without you," he breathed, nudging the tip of her nose with his. "I need you. God...I need you so badly."

Her lips trembled when she lifted her deep, shimmering blue gaze to his. One lone tear spilled down her cheek. "I love you so much, David."

His cock tingled inside her and David knew he wanted to come. At those mere words, he felt his balls constrict and his penis tremble as every muscle in his body stiffened and he was thrust dangerously close to that high point of release. "God, I needed to hear that," he whispered then locked his lips to hers, gently rocking his hips.

He tried to kiss her slowly but he was burning for her, and within seconds the thrusts of his tongue became deep and possessive in her mouth.

Withdrawing his cock, he thrust it briskly back inside her, every muscle straining with effort as he held back his orgasm. He hadn't touched her in over a year and he was so pained his balls were drawn tightly against him. When she made a little sound of pleasure he quickened his pace and found himself sinking his teeth into the flesh of her neck, shuddering at the high, keening sound of her pleasure.

Cupping her breasts, he hauled her back with him as he straightened his spine, her back flattened against his chest as he continued to move inside her. Scraping the pad of his thumb over a rigid nipple, he slid his other hand up her neck, to her jaw. Holding her firmly, he twisted her face so he could kiss her once more. Her lips were soft and moist against his. Drugged by the chocolaty taste of her, he groaned against her lips and drank the sweetness from her mouth. She was his medicine, seeping into his insides until he felt that burning hate easing, soothing, shifting into nothing but love. Desire.

Desperate, he shoved his cock into her body, needing to spill inside her now.

Her face haunted him and suddenly he had to look into those magnificent, electrifying blue eyes. He withdrew from her body, grasped her shoulders and smoothly flipped her back onto the length of the sofa. She was motionless, breathing hard and fast as he placed her legs on either side of his head and positioned himself above her, the back of her knees curving over his shoulders.

Their gazes held, hers brilliant, his dark and pained. In one swift motion he thrust inside her, fully, deeply, completely. She bit her lower lip, whimpering softly, then clutched his hair and pulled him down for her kiss.

She kissed him like she'd die if she didn't, and he welcomed her lips and their generous offering, taking what was given and then some. His teeth gnawed at the tender flesh of her bottom lip, pulling it roughly even as he sped up his thrusts and began to really fuck her, hard and fast.

Within seconds she cried out, her words muffled by his lips, and then he lifted his head and watched the expression on her face as he pummeled inside her. Only when he saw her features tighten and her eyes go blind as she stared up at him, only when he felt her fingers on his head sink viciously into his scalp, did he let loose, let his muscles go and his own orgasm come.

It rocked him completely, every cell in his body shuddering, trembling, exploding along with hers, until he fell limp on top of her.

For a long, breathless moment they lay there, their sweaty bodies entangled. Realizing he was crushing her, David shifted onto his side and dragged her with him until she'd settled comfortably in his arms. Almost in awe, he looked down at her in his arms again. He could hardly keep himself from leaping with joy — but being here with her was infinitely better. She'd snuggled her face against the crook of his neck and her eyelashes rested over her cheekbones as she sighed contentedly.

"Was that good for you, baby?" he whispered softly, planting a gentle kiss on her forehead.

"Hmm," she said in a catlike purr. Then she opened her eyes and regarded him closely. There was a mischievous glint in her gaze when she said, "Let's do that again."

He laughed, a low, rumbling sound that vibrated in his chest then kissed her softly on the lips. "I aim to please."

"In fact, I have a better idea," she suddenly said, twisting her body to rise, making him groan in protest. She came back wiggling the red spin devil in the air, and he immediately glowered at it.

"Not *that* thing again."

She smiled, looking puzzled. "Why not? I think it's cute."

"Yeah, well...I don't trust it."

"It's just a little toy," she said as she pushed a few books to one side of the coffee table so she could set it in the center. Eyeing him in amusement, she arched her brows in a bad imitation of him a while ago and said, "Pitchfork, I get my ring back. Tail, I get my ring back." And then she twirled it.

David laughed when the pitchfork ended up pointing at the bedroom door and the tail toward the opposite wall. Evie's look of disappointment was very apparent—making his heart swell. God, how could he ever live without her? "I told you, that little shit is vicious," he said, rising and hugging her tightly. "You're not getting that ring back, Evie. I'm getting you a new one. This time you can choose it yourself, any ring you want."

"Oh no, you're not. That's not even romantic," she said, shaking her head, her gorgeous locks of black hair flying everywhere.

"If you want romance, I'll give you romance—*right now*, in the bedroom."

He was dead serious. He wanted her again...and he had proof of it if only she'd look down.

She bit back a smile and framed his face with her hands. "If that's your best offer then I guess I'll have to take it."

He bent and kissed her, their lips fusing together gently, lovingly. He'd ached to taste these lips for months and now he couldn't get enough. "I love you, baby."

"Love you too." Her lips curved against his mouth before she pulled away and clamped her hands on her waist. "Then what am I supposed to do with this little friend of yours?" she asked, turning to stare at the intrusive object.

"Pack it up in a box and FedEx it back to Florida. I'm sure Jason would love to have it as a houseguest."

She thought about it for a moment then smiled in agreement. "Just let him know it's coming or he'll probably have no idea what the thing is."

David hugged Evie from behind and rested his chin on her shoulder, his eyes on the devil, his heart in Evie's hands. "Oh believe me, he'll know. He'll recognize the spin devil."

Sending a deadly look its way, he added, "Bon voyage, you stupid little shit."

The End

SPIN SOME MORE

හි

Dedication

∞

I'd like to dedicate this book to the following wonderful people:

To my editor, Kelli Kwiatkowski, for her expertise, dedication and unrelenting faith in me

To my husband, who is simply the most adorable man in the world

And to all my readers, your time and support mean the world to me

From the bottom of my heart, thank you!

Trademarks Acknowledgement

∞

The author acknowledges the trademarked status and trademark owners of the following wordmarks mentioned in this work of fiction:

BMW: Bayerische Motoren Werke Aktiengesellschaft

Care Bears: Those Characters from Cleveland, Inc.

Jell-O: Kraft Foods Holdings, Inc.

PGA Tour: The Professional Golfers' Association of America

Chapter One

ඐ

The spin devil didn't work.

Which was odd, since it was the same toy that had thrown Jason Sheppy and his friends into a sexual frenzy only last year, at their mini-reunion at his beachfront home. Since then, the plush devil had been making the rounds. David had just shipped it to Jason from New York, not having further use for it himself. But now that it was back in Florida, the little bastard wasn't working.

Jason had tried it for the past two weeks and all he'd gotten was a few minutes of lousy sex with a really fat chick. He'd twirled it, whirled it and spun it some more, and no matter whether the tail or the pitchfork pointed at him, he still wasn't getting any hot sex. The conclusion, then, was simple. The little shit didn't work and Jason had no further reason to stride around town looking for a hot date with the little thing sticking from his shirt pocket in case he got lucky — since it was now pretty clear that he *wouldn't*.

He'd been damned glad to see it sink deep into the ocean last night.

The problem was his neighbor, the young and beautiful Penelope Judd, a.k.a. little Miss Disaster, as he liked to think of her, thought she was being very cute and considerate coming to knock on his backdoor the next morning, clutching the vicious little thing in her hands.

Jason didn't know who he was most annoyed at seeing — the spin devil or *her*. Miss Disaster was a load of trouble and every time he had the misfortune of seeing her, she all but dragged him into her personal crap bag of problems. It seemed she always needed someone to do some kind of weird, dirty job for her, and this unfortunate person—without exception—ended up being him.

Only last month, she'd completely lost her house keys only God knows where—and it had probably been on purpose, no doubt, just to give Jason something to yell about. A half-hour later, he'd found himself hanging precariously from the ledge of an open second story window of her house, climbing through it and running down to unlock the front door so the little princess could calmly stride inside. Then last week, she'd crashed her month-old BMW smack center into a palm tree on the side of the road, claiming it had all just "sort of happened." Who did the little troublemaker call? Jason. Hell yeah, why not?

The fact that Miss Disaster had been a permanent resident in his brain for what seemed like forever didn't help his disposition much. Yes, she was damn good-looking, but Penelope was trouble. She was screwing up his brain and messing up his golf.

She was like a child in a woman's body, and he the lucky, lucky sitter.

Two days ago he'd decided to stay away from her from now on because he'd had just about enough. He wanted *nothing* more to do with her. And he'd been doing fine, too, until right now.

He stared her down for a full minute, yet she seemed unperturbed by his deep blue gaze. It was unfortunate that she happened to look extremely, inordinately beautiful this morning, because that meant Jason would have to work double to ignore his body's reaction to her. Her face was all but glowing and the freckles on her nose looked remarkably more like glittering gold than sunspots. Her eyes were framed by thick, spiky lashes and shone a beautiful amber color in the sunlight. Her hair, a soft brown with natural reddish streaks, was held back by a sleek white headband which only served to emphasize the delicate features of her face. Features so angelic that it was hard to believe a real live monster could live under there.

She wore a billowy, long white sundress, the bottom of her skirt flapping softly with the wind and the material around her hips clinging in a way Jason found infinitely disturbing. Flickering gold sandals encased her tiny feet and her little pink toes. Although Jason had never harbored fantasies about licking toes, he found a particularly pleasant one coming to mind. Thank God he quickly caught himself before he did something mental like bite her toe.

In case she didn't get the hint that he was not particularly thrilled to see her, he kept his face masked, his expression solemn. "Penelope," he said flatly, hoping he sounded bored as hell.

Unperturbed by his less-than-warm greeting, she calmly walked past him. "I think you misplaced your toy, Jason," she said airily as she strolled inside, pausing in the middle of the contemporary living room of his beachfront Florida home — a beachfront home which was, because God hated him — right next to hers.

Jason didn't remember ever playing spin devil with her, so how the hell she knew it was his toy, he had no idea.

"Keep it," he said flatly, not wanting to argue with her because he knew it would take up his whole morning, as arguing with her usually did.

"Why would I want to keep it?" She wrinkled her nose, grossed out by the idea. "I'm not a devil worshipper." A wide smile spread her lips, her teeth dazzling white and perfectly straight. "That's why I knew this just *had* to be yours, Jason."

Ignoring her bait, he raked his hands through his hair in exasperation. "Fine, leave it there," he conceded.

Lifting the item in question up to her eye level, she frowned as she scrutinized it. "What's it for anyway?"

"You don't want to know."

Her eyes settled on his for a long, tense moment. Jason had always found that her strange, golden-colored eyes really packed a punch. Every time she locked gazes with him, he felt as if someone had slammed his gut.

"If I didn't want to know I wouldn't have asked you, now would I?"

"It's supposed to be for sex," he said simply. "Not something I want to discuss with you right now."

Her mouth formed a big wide O as her eyes widened. He didn't want to think how damnably sexy she looked, standing in the middle of his living room with her mouth perfectly open and perfectly capable of receiving…something long and hard.

"But…I don't understand… Where are you supposed to put it?" she suddenly asked, acting all innocent and confused. Now *this* was exactly why Jason felt he needed to protect her. She was too naïve, for Christ's sake.

"You twirl it, Penelope. Like a bottle. Ever play spin the bottle?"

"All right then, if you insist. Should I just twirl it right over my palm or…?"

"Do whatever you want with it, I don't really care. Just do it somewhere else."

He knew her so damned well he already knew she'd do the opposite, so he figured he might as well get comfortable. Leaning back on his heels, he crossed his arms and calmly watched as she headed to a nearby table and set it down on top of the gleaming, polished wood.

"Let's see now…hmm…there we go, twirl away little fellow," she said with a wide grin as she spun it. Jason arched a brow when the little thing stopped, the tail pointing straight at him.

"Now what?" Penelope asked, blinking up at him. "Is this where you take your clothes off, or I?"

So witty. So *not* funny. That woman was in sore need of someone tying her to a bed and giving her something to be funny about. She practically lived to taunt and bug him and make him hot and miserable. "This is where you leave," he said coldly.

Finally something got to her, making her little body stiffen. It had been either his tone or the words or both. Whatever. He didn't care to know what, as long as she left him alone.

"Oh, silly me, I keep forgetting how crowded a golfing schedule can be." She snatched the spin devil up to her chest before heading for the door. Pausing when she reached it, she pointed the devil straight at him. "You're being a jerk, Jason." She smiled benignly. "I just thought you'd like to know."

Before she could leave, he snatched her chin with his thumb and forefinger and tilted her face up to his. "And *you're* being a pest." He made an effort not to smile. "I just thought you ought to know."

"Your vocabulary has been very limited lately," she countered, a mischievous spark dancing in her eyes. "That's all you ever call me."

Whenever she smiled at him like that it was as if every organ in his body malfunctioned, and it didn't feel good. Somehow he still managed to shrug, feigning indifference. "I just thought pest sounded a little tamer than *canker*."

She didn't take offense and laughed instead, the sound soft and delicious and totally unfair to him. The way she made him feel—it wasn't pleasant at all. Since she'd become his nightmare of a neighbor over a year ago, the word "peace" had all but gone extinct from his dictionary. Reckless and troublesome as she was, Penelope made his life a real roller-coaster ride. Problem was, Jason wasn't particularly fond of roller-coasters, unless they included an orgasm afterward, which in her case they didn't. All Penelope included in her topsy-turvy adventures was a lousy headache. Or two.

"So," she said merrily. "Any plans after tee time?"

"I'm booked," he instantly said, his eyes falling to her plush, pink lips—lips responsible for plenty of sleepless nights. Nightmares, really. "Big-time booked. Why?"

She shrugged casually. "Oh, I just thought we could play with the devil."

"Don't think so."

She arched her brows. "Why not?" she taunted saucily. "It could be fun. We could—"

"No."

"Jason…"

He grabbed her shoulders and squeezed them hard. "I'm not playing that game."

"But I know for sure you played with Martha the other day!" she protested. "And she said—"

"I don't care what Martha said."

She pursed her lips tightly, her hand coiling around the plush devil's throat as she pressed it to her chest. "Why?" She was squeezing the devil so hard Jason feared the toy's eyes might just pop out any second now. "Why won't you play with me?"

He sighed wearily. Dealing with her was unbelievably draining. "Can't you stop looking for trouble for once in your life?"

"I don't look for trouble, *you* do," she said willfully. "I don't ask you to follow me around. You do that all by yourself."

"I'm saving your ass!" he protested.

"My ass doesn't *need* your precious saving!"

And Jason had already decided that even if it did, he'd save it no more!

When she drew in a deep, miffed breath in a failed attempt to tranquilize herself, her nipples brushed against his chest and he could almost swear she did that on purpose, just to rile him. Jason had never noticed when her breasts had grown, but one day there they were—shouting for attention— and trying not to gape at them had always been exhausting. Her father, being a close family friend, had charged Jason with the noble task of looking out for his youngest daughter, since they'd been friends as kids, and Jason had found he'd taken the task far more seriously than he should have.

Penelope Judd was hardly predictable.

She was quite a little rebel and had been so her whole life. Trouble was as much a part of her as every living inch of her body, and she seemed to love it. The fact that she was reckless, though, didn't mean she was careless. Oh no, Miss Disaster cared about a lot of things. She cared about trash and shopping and making Jason's life miserable.

She was a very caring person when it came to all that. Very thorough and…dedicated.

Shopping. There's a word Miss Disaster understood. To her, it was an art form, a much needed "therapy", which she happened to need often. A couple months ago, right out of the blue, she'd gone shopping for ten hours straight, only to decide to send all her purchases to charity out of damned remorse for spending so much. Jason had wisely suggested she just send the freaking *money* to charity. Did she listen? Oh no, because if it wasn't weird or complicated, it wasn't something Miss Disaster would understand.

Trash. There's another word. Penelope obsessed incessantly about trash and whether some of their nearby neighbors recycled or not. Several weeks ago, she'd volunteered for a local charity that had her picking up litter around the whole freaking town throughout the weekends. Jason wouldn't have minded if it hadn't been for the fact that she'd taken the liberty of signing *him* up as well. So Jason had been picking up trash, watching with a pang of envy as men drove by in their convertibles with hot chicks by their sides, enjoying the good life while *he* got to hang around with the trash girl who was, as one of the local Cubans would put it, a little *loca*.

Penelope's worst obsession though—he was damned sure of it—was him.

Making his life a living hell. She'd been born for it. Making him pick up trash, getting into trouble and creating the need for him to practically baby-sit her every hour of every day. He could hardly stand to be near her anymore. His balls were getting the blues!

Last time she'd invited him for a swim at her place she'd decided to take off her top so she wouldn't get tan lines, and he'd wanted to throttle her with it. Prancing around her pool in a semi-nude state right in front of his startled eyes didn't seem to bother her much, and it drove him insane. The woman was crazy!

Even her very own website design business wasn't enough to divert Penelope's overactive imagination. She still had way too much time on her hands. Jason didn't appreciate having to spend half his days worrying about what trouble she'd get herself into when all he *should* be worried about was beating Tiger Woods at the PGA tour. Instead, he kept fretting over *her*. Her love life. Her whereabouts. The reckless streak she'd given free rein to lately.

She was making him want her—desperately.

And he shouldn't. Not her.

Penelope Judd was just like Eve—but far more innocent and for that reason, all the more dangerous—dangling the dreaded apple in front of him every freaking single day, tempting him to just go ahead and fuck her.

Which of course he wouldn't.

Jason liked his sex naughty, and Penelope Judd had no idea the million things he liked to do to women. She was too young. Too innocent. For God's sake, she'd been playing with Care Bears less than a decade ago, and now she was ready to be tied down and fucked? He didn't think so. Jason was not taking advantage of the twenty-three-year-old handful he'd grown up with—he'd seen her in diapers, for crying out loud.

And despite her being quite a bit of trouble, Penelope was a sensitive, sweet girl and not at all like the groupies with whom he indulged in one-night stands. She was not the kind of woman to take sex lightly. And Jason was only twenty-nine, so he wasn't all that ready for commitment. Not that he'd ever commit to troublesome baggage like her unless he was really, really demented, which he wasn't—at least not yet.

But he was getting there. Thanks to her.

Jason needed to get away from her pronto because he was at the threshold of losing all restraint and doing something really stupid. Getting sexually involved with Penelope was...out of the question.

Not even two years in his new home and he was already considering moving—preferably to another country, or a deserted island, or Saturn even, far, far away from her.

"Don't tell me you're scared of playing a silly little game with me, Jason," Penelope said, her tone light as a summer breeze.

It was hard to maintain the image of a cool, detached male with that last comment. "Look, I'm saving you a whole lot of trouble. The way I see it you should thank me," he said sullenly, roughly scraping his hands up and down her arms.

"The only thing I've got to thank you for is treating me like a child!"

Sighing in defeat, he dropped his hands to his sides. The heat from her body gripped him like a vise, doing unspeakable things to his insides. He could feel parts of his anatomy throbbing, the discomfort in his body gradually intensifying. "I'm looking out for you because it's clear to me that you don't," he tried to explain for the umpteenth time, and for a silly second he was even tempted to agree to play just so he could get rid of her. His palms were starting to sweat and his body was heating up so fast he now also had hyperthermia to worry about.

But she didn't budge an inch, instead tilting her chin up stubbornly. "I think I'm old enough to take care of myself. I'm not five, you know."

"Well I've seen toddlers with more sense than you."

She looked thoughtful for a moment, as if recalling something important. "You know? A lot of men might disagree with that. They think I'm very mature for my age."

Though he knew that was impossible, he nodded just to appease her. "I'm sure they would."

"A lot of men also think I'm really hot," she said matter-of-factly, as if she'd actually conducted interviews.

Jason threw his head back and laughed for a whole minute at that, only sobering up when he suspected, by her narrow-eyed look, that she might actually hit him.

She rose on her tiptoes and glared at him. Jason was a whole head taller than she was and at least double her weight, so that extra inch made absolutely no difference but she obviously thought it did. She actually seemed to think she was intimidating him. "It's not funny, Jason."

He didn't look the slightest bit contrite. "Sorry, but…'hot'? Not really you." He'd go more for "jinxed" or "calamitous" even. He wasn't going to agree she was hot. Not out loud.

She wrinkled her nose at him, her brow furrowing into a scowl—and suddenly she looked ready for a wrestling match. He thought her teeth would crack when she gritted out, "You don't *know* me."

He chuckled softly. "Honey, I know you better than you know yourself."

"You wish you did!"

He shrugged indifferently and said, "Fine. Invite one of your admirers to play then. The ones who think you're so flammable."

She squared her little shoulders. "I think I will," she spat haughtily, all furious now.

She *did* possess that fiery temper redheads were noted for, and it was a joy to watch. Just Jason's way of getting back at her for driving him completely, madly, absolutely insane.

"Now, you're not angry at me are you?" he asked, his voice laced with sarcasm. And now he actually didn't want her to leave. He wanted to fight!

Jason was known to be a patient man, but Penelope had lately been testing him to the breaking point, and fighting with her seemed to be the only non-physical thing he could do with her to get a little release.

"You missed your chance," she spat, her breasts rising and falling at each breath. "Now I won't play with you even if you beg me to!" She threw the door open and all but flew down the wooden planks that led toward the beach.

As if I'd beg her for anything, he thought furiously.

She'd barely hit the sand when he found himself unexpectedly worrying, then cursing under his breath and following her. The truth was, he didn't like pissing her off and he didn't do it on purpose. If only she didn't drive him so frigging nuts! The spin devil in Miss Disaster's hands would be a complete catastrophe—and Jason had to stop her. He had to save her ass, just one last time and that was *it*.

"Penelope," he called after her.

Ignoring him, she lifted the skirt of her dress and trotted across the sand toward her home.

"Penelope," he said again, getting annoyed now.

When he finally reached her, he grabbed her elbow and whirled her around to face him. She yanked her arm free, all fire and haughtiness. Her cheeks were flushed and her breasts rose and fell heavily at each of her breaths.

"I'm just watching out for you," he explained, wishing he could grab her shoulders and shake some sense into her. He'd tried that already, and it didn't work.

113

Her chest heaved, her eyes glowing golden as she looked up at him. "I don't need a watch dog, Jason."

"I'm not a watch dog—I'm your friend," he countered, framing her face with his hands. "Look, that spin devil is serious business."

"And I'm totally up for it!"

"It's wicked."

"Just my kind."

He smiled gently, his eyes filled with concern. "You couldn't be wicked if you tried," he softly said. "Even when you're mean, you're nothing but sweet. Sweet and innocent and…wholesome."

That seemed to hurt her, for her whole body stiffened, her face tinting bright red with fury, easily matching the color of her new little pet. "I hate you!"

"Now, now, Penelope, you're just—"

"And thanks for the toy," she cut in, waving the spin devil in the air. "I'm sure it'll work wonders on a *real* man!" And with that she walked away, leaving Jason staring dumbly after her.

* * * * *

"Yes you are, you're a cute little baby, aren't you?" Penelope cooed to the bundle in her arms as she strode into her spacious two-story beachfront. The adorable plush devil looked right at home in her arms and she could almost swear he winked at her. He liked her coddling, oh yes he did, the little sweetie.

As she headed for the kitchen to separate the cans and plastics she'd recently picked up on the beach—scattered throughout the sand by some insensitive, thoughtless litterbug!—her smile faded as her thoughts returned to Jason.

For the life of her, Penelope had tried and tried to understand Jason, but it was proving to be too damned difficult. The man was impossible! Penelope couldn't comprehend why he didn't want her—it wasn't like him to be so picky.

She'd tried *everything* to lure him. Sunbathing topless, wearing no underwear with her clothes, swaying her hips so hard her spine nearly cracked from the effort. When none of those worked, she'd tried sticking out her butt while bending down to pick up something—something she'd obviously had to drop herself, just to have an excuse to bend over—yet Jason would always find a far more interesting sight than her fanny. Like the ceiling.

When *those* flirtations didn't work, she decided to take a more upfront approach, unashamedly saying things that would leave no doubt whatsoever as to what she wanted. Last week, after they'd laughed for a whole hour during a card game, she'd looked into his eyes and said, "I think I'm hot"— and he'd just swallowed, blinked and then left, the chicken! His attitude was completely baffling, and extraordinarily deflating to a girl's ego. She'd sent him *so* many hints the man had to be an idiot not to get the message, and yet he still refused to make a move on her.

For some reason she couldn't even fathom, Jason still wanted to see her as the vulnerable, skinny little girl he'd grown up with in Miami. How long he planned to treat her like a silly girl, Penelope had no idea, but she was sick and tired of waiting for him to come to his senses. She was *not* sweet and innocent and wholesome, damn it! She was adventurous and impulsive and lately she'd been dying to have sex with him. Maybe it was time to do something drastic, like tie him up and just go ahead and ravage him.

She could've bought any house anywhere in the whole world, and yet she'd bought this one, just so she could be with him and more importantly, to seduce his sorry, playing-hard-to-get ass. A whole lot of good that had done her. She'd made zero progress since moving last year, and during that time, she'd seen her previously active sex life totally dwindle right before her very eyes.

The fact that she wanted Jason so badly had made it pretty hard for her to get laid, especially since every man she met seemed to lack something. Yet the few times she'd been willing to overlook their flaws, the men had either stood her up at the last minute or suddenly backed out—which was most unpleasant. Especially when Jason was getting a lot of attention. Since the day she'd moved here, he'd been getting laid nonstop. Just after moving, she'd snatched up her binoculars during the middle of dinner only to watch slack-jawed as he and his friends fucked right there on the beach. And really? The man was a stallion. It was as if he lazed around all day just to save up his energy for nighttime. He had a sexual appetite bordering on the twisted. And his choices! Why he seemed to want anyone else but her—even Martha, who was older than Penelope's mother and way fatter—was downright mind-boggling.

After his golf tournaments, Jason never hesitated to reach out and grab some groupie's butt or autograph the top of some girl's tit. He totally loved that, and yet when Penelope used her wiles and acted sexy, he completely ignored her and made her feel childish and *so* not sexy.

Well.

Penelope had just about had it. Maybe Jason would like to think of her as this perfect little doll, but damn him, she was flesh and blood too. She had needs, desires, and she'd been so neglected lately she was damn near hospitalization from sheer and utter horniness. She felt so man-starved she'd probably need two dozen men to satiate the hungers in her body.

Penelope was not innocent. Though it had obviously escaped Jason, she'd stopped being a girl the day he'd kissed her cheek while on the swings at the park near her home, when she'd been only twelve. It had been an innocent, brotherly kiss, tender even, but from that day forward she'd been struck with her first and only serious case of puppy love.

116

He'd been eighteen then and already dating—with a vengeance, it sometimes seemed—and Penelope had followed him around like a shadow, vowing one day when she was old enough, *she'd* be the woman in his arms. He'd sometimes let her tag along when he took a girl to the movies or for a burger, and whenever one of his girlfriends had anything negative to say about him bringing Penelope along, he'd dump her. Jason hated complications, so if trouble loomed on the horizon, he'd just quit and move on.

As the years passed and his activities with his girlfriends took a turn for the kinky, Penelope had decided to experiment with boys her own age as she approached eighteen—without her parents' knowledge, of course. Her folks were extremely conservative and had raised Penelope to be a good girl. They were far too old, too, and she didn't want them having heart attacks on her account.

On the night of her eighteenth birthday, Penelope finally went all the way. And rather quickly, sex became surprisingly...addictive. Yet Jason *still* seemed to think that while he was out eating pussy, she was at home playing dress-up or serving tea for her dollies. He was just like her parents, forever thinking she was ten years old.

The fact that she'd become a woman while he was screwing half the country seemed to have completely escaped him. And Penelope wasn't just any woman. She was a woman who'd secretly watched Jason with dozens of others for years, and was more than willing—dying, actually!—to use those same interesting props and gadgets during sex. When would Jason finally realize that she liked to experiment too?

There were a million, zillion things she wanted to do sex-wise...all of them with Jason, and *whomever* he'd want to invite. Yet he looked about as ready to make a move as he had eleven years ago. She knew she *had* to do something to appropriately encourage him. And quickly too—because she couldn't tolerate living with her sexually starved person any longer. It was as if lately she had some sort of infection that made it impossible to get someone in the sack. She was desperate—and no fit company these days.

Perhaps there were women who preferred security and comfort in their lives. Penelope craved excitement, adrenaline and sex. Lots of it. Just like Jason liked it. Tie-me-up sex, bowl-of-Jell-O sex, let-all-our-neighbors-watch sex, smack-my-butt sex, break-the-law sex…just about *any* kind of sex. Yet waiting for Jason to give it to her had proved pretty futile. Well…

Enough of that!

Setting the devil on top of her bed and hoping it would be a good, willing accomplice, she spun it and watched it twirl slowly over her comforter, just a single lazy turn until it halted. The fork pointed straight out her window—toward Jason's place. She stared wistfully at the ignorant little fellow, still damp from when she'd found him on the shore this morning. "I don't think Jason's willing, little friend." Then she grinned down at it. "But don't worry, I'm sure there are plenty of men who'd want to play with us," she said encouragingly.

Sitting on the edge of the bed, she pulled out a brown leather book from the nightstand, reached for the phone and dialed.

She went through every number of every single man she knew, ones she'd never quite managed to sleep with and others who'd already shown her a good time.

It was starting to seem extremely odd that none of them seemed interested.

Until Bob Farley said over the phone, "I'd be there in an instant, Penny, but that friend of yours seemed really pissed the last time I was by your place, and he's a little too much for me to handle, you know?"

"Who is?" she asked dumbly.

"Your neighbor. The golfer. Asked me not to come around again—and he didn't ask me nicely."

For a few seconds, she was rendered speechless. "Do you mean Jason?"

"The blond guy who's been playing like shit for the past year?"

"Yes." Penelope felt lightheaded, and had to place a steadying hand on her forehead.

"Then that's him all right."

"But why would he do that?" she asked in a tiny voice, bubbles of fury simmering in her stomach.

"I don't know, sweetheart, I didn't hang around long enough to ask, you understand. But why don't you ask him?"

"I'll *kill him*, is what I'll do! Is that why Tom stood me up too?"

"Tom? Oh no," Bob said, laughing on the other end. "Tom got it much worse. That Jason is one hell of a jealous bastard, sugar. Look, you know how hot I think you are and everything…"

She didn't hear the rest. She dropped the receiver to her lap and stared down at it in horror. Faintly, she could still hear Bob's voice rambling on, but her mind was racing and her heart was pounding a mile a minute.

She would kill him, the bastard. Jason was scaring away her men! And how on Earth did he manage to see Bob Farley that night? Bob never even rang the doorbell—he'd stood her up! Was he actually…?

Oh, but of course he was. Jason was *spying* on her!

How *dare* he, the creep?

True, she'd spied on him too, but she'd never interfered with his dates, even if most times she would've been doing him a great favor.

After muttering a quick farewell and hanging up, she furiously flipped through the phone book. If Jason was spying on her, then she really ought to give him something to look at. *Of course* he'd been thinking she was innocent—he was damned well making sure of it, wasn't he? *Well, we'll see about that*, Penelope thought smugly.

Pausing at a page, she grunted in pleasure at her find and dialed the number of the one place Jason would never suspect she'd look for a partner.

"Hi, is this the Better Have male escort service? I need an escort for tonight."

Chapter Two

ஐ

That afternoon, while staring blankly down at his sand wedge and playing the worst eighteen holes of his life, Jason received a package.

"Mr. Sheppy?" a young man asked, and Jason nodded. He wore no uniform, and Jason could only deduce the guy had been hired by some shy, star-struck fan.

After hesitantly taking it, he watched the boy leave before tearing the box open, pulling out a pair of white, lacy female underwear and a pair of binoculars with a yellow note.

Innocent? Watch me!

He stared down in puzzlement at the binoculars then at Miss Disaster's underwear, telling himself he would *not* smell them in front of his caddy. Then he thrust both into the outer pocket of his golf bag, zipped it shut and continued down the fairway and on to the next hole. Plugging in the tee, he found himself staring blindly down at the golf ball and wondering what in the hell the little monster was scheming now.

He had absolutely no idea and it made him scowl down at the turf, take a lousy swing and miss. Mumbling a curse, he ignored his caddy's telling cough and resumed his position again. What he *did* know for sure was that Miss Disaster wouldn't be playing spin devil tonight. Pretty much the entire male population of Florida had been warned, so the little miss would shockingly discover she had no one to play with. So unfortunate for her.

Jason knew Bob Farley wouldn't dare say yes unless he wanted to find his teeth in the next block. Hudson was too vain to want to get his nose cracked. Tom, Oliver and Trent, they'd never risk getting Jason's five-iron up their asses. And if some bastard with a sudden case of amnesia dared say yes, at least the spin devil hadn't been very effective recently.

It damned well better not start now.

After showering at the club and changing into a clean pair of khaki shorts and a white polo, Jason headed straight home. As soon as he got to his beachfront, he glanced down at his watch, noting it was 8:55 p.m., and took the staircase two steps at a time up to his bedroom. Dropping the binoculars on his bed—because he didn't need those—he crossed his room toward the full-size telescope by the window.

He'd bought it just to watch her. Yes, that was sick, and it had been damned expensive too, but heck, Jason needed to look after her. Make sure there was no one there who shouldn't be. Make sure she was okay. That was the sole purpose of the telescope—to protect her.

And maybe watch her sometimes at night while she slept, make sure no robbers or burglars were prowling about. No nighttime lovers.

Whenever he watched her at night, she looked like an angel sleeping over a cloud...lying on her side, little hands tucked under her cheek. He'd tortured himself often, imagining those eyes fluttering open before she pulled back the sheets and welcomed him into her bed. He'd have to say no...right? Because she was too vulnerable, and Jason wasn't sure if he could be tender and sweet with someone he'd wanted for so long—he liked BDSM, he liked kinky and he liked variety. Penelope was precious and fragile. And his friend. He'd only end up hurting her. He wouldn't be able to live with himself if he ever hurt her. Hell, if anyone hurt her. The thought of another man touching her had always driven him out of his mind. He'd told himself repeatedly that when a worthy candidate came along, he was going to have to leave them be—but damn it, no one deserved her at all!

Penelope was pretty selective about her shoes, yet when it came to men, she dated the most hotheaded assholes *ever*. If it weren't for Jason, who'd been pretty damned efficient in keeping the men away, she'd have a heartache for every month of the year. That wasn't something he was willing to allow. No one was going to use her for sex — or anything else, for that matter. Not Jason, and certainly not some other asshole.

Keeping his bedroom lights off, Jason positioned the telescope, aiming it toward the front door first and leaning close to take a look, checking for any parked cars nearby. Satisfied there weren't any, he shifted it toward her window. Darkness hung over the beach like a shroud, the blackened sky clear and speckled with stars.

The same instant his eye focused on her window, the curtains to her bedroom slid open. Her room was bathed in warm light and she was there, centered in the window, her loose auburn hair tumbling past her shoulders.

His cock stiffened and he swore under his breath when he noted the sexy, nearly nonexistent number she was wearing. Black. Very sheer and very short, not even reaching thigh.

Jason certainly hadn't seen *that* little number before. It had been made for her, tailored to perfection. God, she had the body of a centerfold. Sleek and curvy. He could see her full, round breasts under the sheer fabric. And if he looked lower...

What the hell did she want to do, give him a goddamned heart attack? She was wearing no panties! Her pussy was about the most tempting thing he'd seen in his life — a perfect short line of trimmed auburn hair that disappeared temptingly between her legs.

He'd wondered about it so many times, his knees felt weak now that he realized he couldn't have begun to imagine anything as perfect. Was he supposed to forget that image next time he saw her, damn it? Panting for air, he pulled away and glared at the telescope, certain the thing had just scorched his eyeball. Penelope was punishing him, damn her perverted little ass. Now what else did she have in store, besides this little striptease? Innocents weren't supposed to do that! What in the hell was wrong with her? Didn't she recall she was

Penelope Judd—not a femme fatale, not some groupie, not a sex-bomb?

Holding his breath until his lungs stung, he bent to take another look. She was dragging a chair and placing it before the window. Then she sat back and remained very still, her eyes fixed straight on him, as if she had a superhuman eye and could miraculously see all the way into his room. His muscles tightened with need—one in particular more than the others.

Gracefully, as if she'd done this a million times, she lifted the sheer little thingy up past her stomach and parted her legs. Jason felt dizzy. Her pussy was swollen and pink and so damned wet that it glistened. He licked his lips as he watched her rub the tip of one finger over her clit, delicately moving it in slow, dizzying circles. He hissed out a breath when she briskly thrust the full length of her finger inside her.

Hunger tightened her face, her eyes slamming shut, her forehead creasing with a desire so fierce that it looked almost painful. Jason couldn't take it—he'd been suffering with this need for months. Years even. It was so damned hard not to want her, especially when she was in every dream, in the back of his mind every time he fucked someone. Groaning a choked, pained sound, he grappled with his shorts and underwear, dropping them to his ankles so he could fist his cock.

He curled his fingers around himself and slowly began to stroke, his watchful eye on her. She was screwing two fingers inside her pussy now, her legs spread so wide she'd draped the back of a knee over each armrest. Jason squeezed the base of his cock then stroked upward, tightening his hold when he reached the head, all the while caressing his scrotum with his other hand, fiddling with his balls. She suddenly pulled the nightie over her head then grabbed something from nearby. A pink, silicone dildo. Where the hell did she get that?

She held it with steady hands, as if it were no stranger to her, and the truth of the matter was, the woman looked anything but sweet now. She looked burning, sizzling hot, and this time he found nothing laughable in it. Damn her, she made him want her so bad. Why was she torturing him like this? This past year had been hell! He'd been going haywire trying not to notice her "charms", particularly since a good part of the time they were so obviously on display for him.

But there was no harm in looking now, was there? He was more than a hundred yards away, his lights were off and the night was conveniently black, with no moon to disclose him or his intentions. No one ever need know, and if she asked, he could always pretend he hadn't seen anything...

So he watched, fevered with arousal, as she rubbed the tip of the cock between the heavy globes of her breasts before moving it lower. Oh God, he might even die watching—and a sweet death it would be.

Yeah, go on, slide it into that pussy, baby...

Her mouth parted and she let out a moan he imagined he could hear as she thrust that fake dick into her pussy. Jason shuddered, delirious as he noted the pleasure that flashed on her face as she fucked herself with that huge dildo. He fervently wished it was him. He wished he owned that fucking cock and was buried deep inside her, deep inside that wet, slippery, tight-as-ass cunt of hers.

She withdrew the dildo and brought it to her mouth, tasting her juices on the tip of it with her tongue then dipping it fully past her lips and into the hot, wet cave of her mouth.

Suck it, baby, suck it hard, Jason urged mentally as he watched her, his strokes quickening on his cock, his other hand harshly squeezing his nuts, tearing a low, anguished sound from his chest. Jason actually liked squeezing his balls, liked to feel pain when he was aroused—stark, naked pain that only enhanced his pleasure.

He'd never burned this way, as if any minute now his skin would turn to ashes. He'd never felt so hot, so damned horny, as he felt now, watching her masturbate, watching her shove that huge fake cock into her mouth while he jerked off.

He was about to come, just watching her suck that cock while she stroked her clit with her other hand.

Stick it inside…stick it into that sweet, tight cunt, baby…

She guided the dildo through the parted seams of her sex, using both hands to push the shaft inside and judging by the look on her face, another moan seemed to tear out of her, making Jason groan deep in his throat and pinch his own scrotum while he tightened his hold around himself.

He was going to come. He was going to explode like he'd never before—

But then something happened. She paused and turned her head to stare at something past her shoulder.

And then Jason saw him.

His hands stilled on his privates, a frown settling on his face.

Some man, a stranger, crossing the room toward her. Someone big, muscular and young. Jason gritted his teeth as he watched him stride with a lazy swagger toward the window and slowly pull the curtains closed.

Son of a bitch!

* * * * *

"Excuse me?"

"I asked if you'd like to sit down," Penelope repeated as she slipped the sheer black nightie over her head again.

"Sure."

The male escort from the highly recommended Better Have escort service slowly sat on the end of the bed. He was very handsome, with dark brown hair and warm brown eyes. His skin was smooth and tanned, and although Penelope thought he might be a little too muscular for her tastes, he was big and strong and two grand said he had to be *very* well endowed. He was wearing tight jeans and an even tighter red

T-shirt and he looked just about ready for sex — which Penelope really appreciated.

"So, Murry, right?" she asked calmly.

"Right."

"So, tell me about yourself. Do you have any brothers, sisters?" she prodded, her smile sincere as she grabbed the chair she'd placed before the window and turned it around to face the bed behind her. Sitting down, she crossed her legs with a swift, elegant move.

"Umm, yeah, I got three sisters."

"How nice."

"Yeah."

Silence ensued, making Murry notably uncomfortable. He rushed to fill it. "I think that's why I'm so in tune with what women need, with what they want. I'm very in touch with my feminine side," he proudly said.

"Of course you are," she soothed.

"I can always go both ways. Know what I mean?" He eyed her when she remained silent. "Um. You wanna start with this?" he suddenly asked, looking puzzled.

"I was wondering if we could play a little game." She smiled and glanced at the red toy devil on her nightstand. "See that little devil there? We spin it, like a bottle, and whoever gets the pitchfork gets to dare the other. I'm sure we can come up with all kinds of dares, aren't you?"

There was a loud, obvious sound of a door slamming shut on the first floor.

"Oops," Penelope said, her eyes widening in surprise. "I think I know who *that* is." And she could hardly believe her good fortune!

"Huh?" Murry asked, clearly confused.

She shooed her hands, hurrying him. "Now, if you will kindly remove your clothes and maybe do a little dance for me in your underwear, I'm sure it will help a lot."

"Um…"

"Quickly!" she urged.

He was out of his clothes within seconds, and then began a slow, shake-your-booty dance in red thong underwear that appropriately displayed his tight buttocks and lovingly hugged his big package like a second skin. Penelope pasted a besotted smile on her face as she watched him until finally the door to her room burst open and there he was.

Jason Sheppy.

Penelope's heart did a double-flip, the blood suddenly rushing through her veins in an avalanche. He looked so gorgeous and so…*positively jealous*. She'd never expected such excellent results from this impulsive plan of hers. She'd dearly hoped he might feel inclined to attend the game after all, but with Jason's stubbornness, his reaction had been quite unpredictable. He was always so lazy and carefree. She knew how much he hated to have to work hard to achieve anything, and it was always up to Penelope or his golfing coach to pressure him to give his best. Well. Tada.

Penelope was getting his best tonight.

Actually, he seemed a little agitated. He was panting like a bull, hands clenched into fists at his sides, thick cords straining in his neck. His eyes were narrowed and glimmering menacingly at poor old Murry, who was still doing his little routine for her, shaking his butt with his hands placed behind his head, twirling all over the room as if any minute now she'd slip a dollar into his shorts.

"Get the hell out of here!"

Even Jason's voice, usually casual and level, was now craggy and harsh. As if she completely missed the threat underlying his tone, Penelope smiled reassuringly at Murry, who turned to her with a quizzical expression on his face.

"Oh, never mind him," she explained gently, waving a hand in dismissal. "Drop your underwear, please."

Murry hooked his thumbs to the sides of his underwear and pulled it down while Jason's whole body shook gravely with obvious consuming rage that tinted every inch of his skin a deep red color. He looked ready to murder someone—or maybe ready to fuck her, at long, long last.

"I said *leave*, goddamn it, before I do something violent!"

"Jason!" Penelope chided, outraged. "You're going to have to wait your turn. I'm paying a good two-thousand dollars for this lover boy here, and I'll be damned if he leaves without giving me a much-needed orgasm."

Jason glowered at Murry, who was now completely naked, his soft cock dangling before him like a large, lazy elephant trunk, and Penelope felt *very* pleased with the evident envy on Jason's face when he noticed. Then his anger seemed to intensify to magnificent proportions. His features suddenly twisted, nearly deformed with rage.

She found it terribly amusing.

That is, until his eyes landed on her—and the look in them was unquestionably deadly. Fear whipped inside her. He was not furious at the escort, she suddenly realized.

"What do you think you're doing?"

His hoarse voice vibrated with a muted but unmistakable sound of rage. Penelope gripped the chair armrests and kept her smile in place even if it might cost her dearly. Her insides were in turmoil. Her heart felt crowded with so much desire but now also with just a bit of fear. She had never seen him like this. Jason always seemed so cool. "I thought you'd like to watch him *play* with me," she said casually. "Since you're so good at spying and everything, and I'm no better than a toddler as far as you're concerned."

He walked toward her with slow, sure footsteps, his eyes almost murdering her on the spot. "You little *bitch*."

She sighed dramatically, fighting to appear calm. "Now that was uncalled for, Jason. I thought you said I was wholesome."

"And are you really?" When Jason reached the chair, he grabbed her arms and pulled her up, his lips only a breath from hers. "You're testing my nerves, Penelope. I've a mind to fuck your brains out and give you what you deserve."

Her heart raced with excitement. Finally. Finally! He was going to fuck her brains out. "No one's stopping you," she whispered.

"Did you honestly think I was going to stand there and watch while some bastard fucked you?"

"Well you've never shown much interest in doing it yourself, so I just figured—"

"*Damn you*! I was protecting you! From men like *him*—and men like *me*!"

His biceps bulged and rippled as he threw her down on the bed. She bounced once before instinctively backing away, only to notice he was stripping off his clothes. "Damn it all to hell now. If you want to be used, fine, then *I'm* the one who'll be using you!" He was shaking with rage as he undressed while she watched in fascination, her eyes greedily absorbing every newly revealed inch of bronzed, bare skin.

"You're wrong, Jason," she finally said. "You see...*I'm* the one who's going to be using *you*."

"Is that right?" He slowly approached her, his angry eyes piercing to her insides like blue lasers. "*Never* start a game you don't know how to play, Penelope."

He was fully naked now, and she had only a few precious seconds to marvel at how utterly beautiful his body was, all those sleek, tanned muscles. Not thick like Murry's, but sinewy and hard. There was a faint tan line around his hips and for a moment she wished she could ask him to turn around so she could stare at what had to be a glorious, rock-hard butt. Instead, her eyes bulged at the front view. His cock was huge, throbbing, straining up toward the ceiling with pride. "Your little game is over. Now we're playing *my* way."

She could tell he was going to ravage her. Yes, he was — and he couldn't do it fast enough to suit her.

"Take off that thing."

Penelope didn't need to be asked twice. She briskly pulled off her sexy sheer baby-doll, watching his reaction as she flung it aside. Her nakedness didn't seem to appease his anger much but his eyes suddenly glowed with heat. Murry took a seat on the chair Penelope had previously occupied, his cock now fully erect as he sank back to watch.

"Open your legs."

Penelope held her breath. Jason's blue eyes — dark and deadly and right on target — fixed hungrily on the apex of her legs as she slowly parted them.

"Touch it. Touch your pussy."

Penelope's insides quivered as she slowly brushed her hand down her belly, grazing past the trimmed hairs until she held herself, hot and wet and ready in her palm.

"Spread your lips apart so I can see right into you."

Spreading two fingers to each side of her labia, she pulled her lips wide. Growling in hunger, his cock quivering in his excitement, Jason bent forward, inching his face toward her pussy. She gasped when he licked her, like a dog, just one quick, fast lick inside the folds of her sex, making her moan for more. He pulled back slightly and stared, dark-eyed, right into her cunt as she held her entrance wide apart with her fingers.

Ten long heartbeats later, he finally dipped his head, his tongue gently lapping at her pussy. Biting her lower lip with a muffled cry, she shoved her hips up to his mouth, urging him to thrust his tongue deeper and lick and eat it all. His tongue followed the silent command, swiftly dipping inside.

That thick, hot tongue was thorough, a master of seduction as it rubbed the swollen muscles of her cunt, making her juices flow like warmed honey. She shivered under the slow, sensual strokes and stared unseeingly up at the ceiling, never having imagined his tongue could feel so wonderful.

"Where's that plastic cock?" Jason asked, his voice harsh with need.

"On the table, beside the chair," she said breathlessly, seizing the brief moment to try to steady her breath. He quickly grabbed it and handed it to her, his face tight with arousal.

"Put it inside you."

She took it in her hands, hesitating for a moment.

"Put it inside you and masturbate. I want to see you."

There was determination in his voice, but she shook her head. "No, I want *you*, Jason. It's you I —"

"Hush." He pressed a finger to his own lips, his jaw held so tight his teeth could've cracked. "Just do it."

She closed her eyes, raising her hips as she thrust the dildo inside her, hissing out a sharp breath when it filled her.

Her eyes opened to find Jason standing before the bed, enveloping the length of his cock in his hands, his whole attention focused on her as he began to squeeze himself. Murry was busy behind him, pulling hard at his cock, breaths short and fast.

Penelope met Jason's gaze while she slowly continued to play with herself, pressing that dildo in deeper, slipping it out then back in again. It stretched the walls of her cunt so wide she thought it would break her in half, but still she wanted more, couldn't push it deep enough.

Glancing down at Jason's dick, her eyes misted with desire as she saw how slowly he stroked himself, rocking his hips while he did so, now cupping his testicles with his other hand. Using the binoculars, she'd once seen him masturbate over his bed while watching a porn movie. She had been so aroused just by watching him. But now, hearing the low, ragged sounds of his breathing, smelling the musky male scent of his arousal and sensing the warmth of his body so near, watching simply could not compare.

Jerking her hips upward, she pushed the dildo farther inside her, now oblivious to everything except the sweltering heat and the acute pain between her legs. She was moaning loudly, and she heard other sounds in the room too. Low, guttural sounds coming from Jason and deep, hungry groans coming from Murry. All three of them made agonized, delirious sounds of pleasure to create a hot, dark symphony that seemed to echo in the room.

Jason pulled at his cock, jerking it arduously, sweat beading his brow as he watched her lift her hips to receive the dildo up to her core, fully, completely. Her breasts bounced at the force of her thrusts, jerked and jiggled as she moved. When that tension, that promising pain became unbearable, she cried out and shuddered at the same moment his semen shot in the air and his body shook in tremors.

The escort screamed behind them, coming loud and hard in a shattering earthquake that could've shaken the floor beneath them.

A deathly silence descended over the room the next minute, stark and dreary compared to the wanton music that had preceded it. When Penelope finally recovered, she lazily sat up on the bed, meeting Murry's warm brown gaze and crooking her finger at him with a wicked glint in her eye. "Come here, big boy."

Jason frowned, his biceps clenching with tension as Murry stepped forward. Penelope eyed Murry's member as if she were a scientist studying something of critical consequence. Smiling in satisfaction, she cupped his dick in her hand and immediately, as if by magic, it thickened and hardened under her palm. Thrilled, she glanced up and smiled at him. "Nice. *Very* nice. Do you actually take something to perform adequately, or how do you get hard so soon after...?"

"Some guys take a few pills but I'm a natural," Murry admitted softly, his cheeks staining bright pink.

"Keep your hands to yourself, Penelope," Jason growled, his eyebrows furrowing into a scowl, his hands fisting at his sides.

She giggled and dropped her hand. "Fine. No hands." Falling back on the bed, she had eyes only for Murry. She'd intended to give Jason a show and now he would get it. "How about fucking me with no hands? Think you can manage? Just your cock, nothing else can touch me."

Jason watched, seemingly stupefied while the muscled escort gently shouldered him aside and knelt on the bed as Penelope parted her legs wide so he could slide his hips between her thighs. She gasped when he entered her, glorying at the feel of his hardened cock inside her. Their bodies were joined only in that single place, his cock slowly sinking into the pink, slippery slit between her legs.

Every one of her senses felt attuned to that pulsing male organ entering and withdrawing from her heat. It felt so sensual, to touch only in that place, his gentle penetration heightening the sensitivity of her pebbled flesh and the feel of each little quiver in her cunt as it squeezed and drew his cock farther inside her. Murry made a low, gruff sound and Penelope closed her eyes and arched her back, ripples of pleasure washing over her as he began a slow, leisurely fuck.

* * * * *

Jason was going to fucking *kill* her—but first he was going to watch. Oh dear Lord. Dear, dear Lord. She was going to be the end of him.

His eyes dropped to her tits. They called to him, round and full and female, the nipples drawn and puckered for his kiss already. Moving to the side of the bed, he bent forward, drawing one nipple into his mouth, laving it with his tongue. When it was wet and quivering, he suckled it. Her whole body trembled under his lips and he suckled harder, using his teeth to nip the hard little crest, wanting to devour her. Milk her.

Huffing, puffing sounds reverberated in the room as Murry fucked her—no hands, just cock—and Jason was so fevered and frantic and wanting that he'd never thought such ardent need possible.

When Murry began to ram inside Penelope's small, sleek body even faster, making her whimper and cry like a mare, Jason knew he couldn't stand it anymore. He needed to be inside her, in that place he'd always craved, a place he knew in his heart was *his*.

He leaned close to whisper to her. "Suck him," he ordered, hungrily dipping his tongue in her ear.

Penelope opened her eyes to stare hazily up at Murry. "Come here and let me suck you, big boy," she said in an intimate whisper.

When Murry moved, Jason immediately took his place, grabbing Penelope's hips and sinking his fingers into her warm, moistened flesh as he slammed inside her, making a loud, deranged sound when his penis was finally—*finally*, after years—fully sheathed inside her.

Murry slowly lay down on the bed beside her, settling his hips a few inches away from her face. As if starved, Penelope opened her mouth and searched for the thick, bulbous head of his cock, purring in pleasure when she found it and tugging it into her mouth with her lips. Frenzied, she looked desperate to eat it, taking as much of it as possible while Jason fucked his way into her pussy.

Jason watched her take the other man, watched as her mouth parted wide and her tongue rubbed against the length of Murry's thick organ, flicking the folds of the head, swiping along the tip. Licking every inch of his cock that she could, her hand gently cupped his nuts, her thumb slowly brushing along the sparse hairs over the sac, making him groan deliriously.

Jason was mad with need, his grip holding her fast as he screwed her at will, pounding his cock deep inside her, pulling it out wet and slick and gleaming with her cream, then ramming it back in. No one made him this hot, this horny, except this innocent little slut, doing all these naughty things to him. Torturing him, tormenting him—and proving that she was even wilder than he was!

Her cunt squeezed him, slick and tight, like nothing he'd slipped his cock into before. If she weren't sucking on Murry he'd want to pull out his cock and make her suck it, make her taste her own pussy on him, make her eat his drops of cum and lick every inch of his dick.

"Do you like it?" he asked thickly, his voice heavy with arousal. "You like sucking cock?"

She tilted her head back to whisper a low and sultry, "Yes," before taking the cock greedily into her mouth again, drinking from it as if it were her life's sustenance, as if she couldn't live without it or bear a minute away from it.

Jason groaned and cupped her breasts as he moved his hips back, gently withdrawing, only to slam back inside her again. Murry's body tensed as he neared his climax and he pulled out of her mouth. Penelope curled one hand around him and began to stroke him fast.

Jason went crazy, his lungs exerting as they fought for air while he pounded into her cunt as if the devil himself were forcing him to.

Penelope shuddered just as she opened her mouth, slid out her tongue and caught some of Murry's cum as he exploded, spilling his cream. She drank most of it, purring in delight, while the rest fell on her chin and lips, where she licked it ravenously, making Jason the hottest, horniest bastard in the whole hot-damned world. He came inside her with a harsh cry of passion, shuddering completely before he fell beside her on the bed, limp and nearly, *very* nearly, dead.

Chapter Three

❧

For a few moments they said nothing and just lay there, the three of them, entangled on the bed. Chest heaving, Jason stared up at the ceiling and reached out to stroke Penelope's naked, sweaty body lying motionless beside his. "Wow. That was just...wow!" Jason said dazedly, still feeling winded.

"Uh-huh," came Murry's reply.

Jason lifted his head and glowered at him across the peaks of Penelope's nipples. "Don't you think it's about time you left already?"

Murry propped himself up on an elbow and stared down at Penelope. "Should I?"

Biting back a smile, she shook her head solemnly as she sat up on the bed. "No, please don't, because I have one itty-bitty request from you. From *both* of you, actually."

Jason inwardly groaned. Oh no. Penelope's requests were usually flat-out horrifying, like that time she'd asked him to rescue an already dead animal from the street and drive for miles just to get to a vet to see if a resuscitation was possible — which of course Jason knew was not. His car had stunk for weeks.

"That is," Penelope added teasingly, switching her gaze from one man to the other. "*If* you can both get it up."

"Of course," Murry quickly assured.

Jason's scowl intensified. Was this a challenge? Would it mean he wasn't man enough if he didn't get it up for the third fucking time in one single night? He relaxed only slightly when he realized maybe poor Murry wouldn't be so eager to get it up if he knew what sort of discomforting "requests" Penelope usually thought up.

"Jason?" she prodded.

He sighed. "All right, what?" he heard himself say.

"Could you guys stand together and…rub cocks for a few minutes?"

Jason jackknifed to a sitting position. "*What*?"

Penelope smiled at him charmingly, clasping her hands before her chest as if in prayer. "Oh puleeeze?"

"Of course by all means *no*!" Jason immediately said, bounding up from the bed with record speed.

Penelope giggled, eyes twinkling. "I just want you to rub your cocks together and let me watch just a little. I'd really like that."

Jason looked at her from across the room as if she'd grown lizards on her head. He shook his head in disbelief. "Baby, you're really scaring me."

"I told you I could be wicked. Well, there you have it. It's my own very secret, very *private* fantasy."

Smiling, she pushed herself off the bed and walked toward him, swaying her hips slowly, like a sultry goddess of sex. "Would you be willing to grant me this little wish, Jason? I'd be happy to make any of *yours* come true."

She knew just how to ask him, damn her, but this time it was not going to happen. "Yeah, baby, but…"

"Come on, man," Murry said, rising from the bed. "We'll just rub cocks, have some rowdy fun."

Jason stared pointedly at Murry's already-hard, magical, ever-stiff cock. "I hardly think that would be fun," he said seriously.

"It's just rubbing cocks, handsome, it's not anything drastic," Penelope encouraged.

"The hell it's not!"

She crossed her arms and shrugged. "Fine, then don't."

"Maybe if we spin the toy like you said..." Murry intervened behind her, grabbing the spin devil from the nightstand and waving it in the air.

Penelope whirled to face him, smiling. "Murry, you are absolutely brilliant."

If that comment wasn't infuriating, Jason didn't know what was. He glowered as Murry set the thing on the stand and sent it spinning. "I'm not rubbing cocks no matter what that damned toy—"

"Fork!" Penelope squealed, the tips pointing right at Jason.

Murry looked confused. "Does fork means I get to rub cocks with him?"

"No!" Jason snapped at the same time Penelope said, "Yes!"

Jason pursed his lips as she turned to face him. She was flushed, smiling and looking all lovey-dovey. In fact, she was looking up at him in the same damned way she always did when she wanted to get her way. It was the puppy-dog-behind-the-window-of-the-pet-shop look. Damn her.

Damn her *twice* because he actually felt himself responding to her ridiculous request.

His cock hardened at her pleading look, hardened at the pleasure the mere thought of pleasing *her* gave him. Hardened at the mere thought of doing something really...very...disgustingly...*kinky*.

"Goddammit," he grumbled, and before he thought better of it, he walked toward Murry, thinking he'd make damned sure his friends never, *ever* found out about this. Jason was no man-lover. He'd get ribbed for all eternity for sure. Glancing down to check his tool, he stared at Murry's, then at his again, trying to discern if he was at least the bigger of the two.

It was a close call. Actually maybe Jason lost by a hairbreadth...or a tiny bit more. Aw shit, the man's cock was really big. But he was a freaking pro! He *lived* to fuck.

While Jason *loved* to fuck, he was hardly a gigolo. And his cock was real—no enhancing anything. Unlike whatever Murry obviously did to his. He didn't buy that "natural" thing for a second.

Cheating bastard.

* * * * *

Barely able to believe this wasn't a dream, Penelope took a step back and felt a crashing wave of desire flood between her legs as she watched both men slowly move forward. They were the same height, and although Murry's cock was about half an inch longer, Jason's was thicker, smoother. More beautiful than anything to her.

Their foreheads almost made contact when they both stared down and watched in fascination as their tall, throbbing cocks crowded the space that separated them. When they actually touched, the men's bodies stiffened…maybe in shock, maybe in arousal.

Yes, definitely in arousal, for both their breaths quickened harshly…

Then they began to rub. First just the tips of their cocks, head against head, the bulbous mushrooms slowly stroking against each other. Then, ever so slowly, the whole thick length of them, rubbing up and down, skin to skin.

There was a low, soft brushing sound in the room as their flesh rubbed. Blood pulsed inside their members and even as they touched, both their dicks seemed to throb and tremble in need. Less hesitant now, the men moved closer and scraped their dicks more forcefully, as if their cocks were pained and itching for a scratch. Brazenly, they guided their cocks up and down, now oblivious to Penelope's presence as they gazed down at themselves, at the way their cocks scraped and brushed and rubbed.

Suddenly, as if in accord, their bodies strained closer, their dicks pressing tightly, their balls almost touching. They were so close, their privates smashed together and appearing almost as one, that it was hard to see where one male began and the other ended.

Penelope's insides felt like molten lava. An acute, sizzling pain clenched inside the walls of her cunt like a fist of fire. She felt fevered, euphoric, to watch the man she'd always dreamed of do this for her, do this because she was a wicked little girl, repressed her whole life, and had let her inner harlot out to play.

She slowly slid a finger inside her and bit back a moan, not wanting to distract the two males, not wanting to miss a precious moment of this wild, wicked fantasy. Her sex was hot, almost scorching the flesh of her finger as she planted it as deeply as she could. She watched as Murry grabbed Jason's shoulders and pulled him closer until their chests pressed together. Rocking his hips against Jason's, their cocks full and hard and throbbing, Murry growled.

Muscles rippling, Jason put his hands on Murry's hips and began to rock his own, his buttocks flexing at his moves. The tips of their cocks glistened with cum and Penelope knew they were finding pleasure in her request. They were both breathing harsh and fast, like two gnarly beasts mating, and they looked more than ready to get down to business and fuck.

Soundlessly walking forward, she placed a gentle hand on each man's ass, simultaneously squeezing their flesh before shifting her hands, dipping a finger between each of their buttocks until she was stroking their hot, puckered anuses. Her hardened nipples lightly brushed against the side of their chests. Their hot, rapid breaths fanned her face. Each breath they took became louder, deeper as they hastened to rub more fiercely now, their chests pressing tightly, more cum glistening from the tips of their cocks. She stroked both their anuses, suddenly inserting the tip of a finger inside each.

Sweat glistened on his brow as Jason turned his head and kissed her, sticking his tongue into her mouth. Groaning in pleasure, Murry joined the kiss, sliding his tongue inside her parted lips until all three tongues blended together along with the mingled taste of their saliva, their ragged breaths and their needy, animal noises. When she pulled away, she watched, mesmerized, as the men continued the kiss for a few endless seconds, their tongues tasting and feasting together. Jason growled deeply, as if he liked the kiss and the taste of Murry's mouth.

Murry ground his cock against Jason's, chafing himself against him as if desperate to come, come over Jason and spill himself on another man's cock.

Penelope's legs shook as she moved back to sit on the edge of the bed, spreading her legs wide open and touching the quivering nub of her clit as she watched. No civilized men were in this room tonight. They were just animals now, wanting to fuck something, someone, whoever, whatever it was.

"I could fuck you," Murry whispered against Jason's lips, sounding more than a little aroused. "Fuck you good and hard."

Jason stared back at him panting, a look of uncertainty crossing his face before he turned to meet Penelope's gaze. Their eyes locked. Holding her breath, she nodded pleadingly, thinking there would be nothing more exciting to her than watching a man taking Jason while he fucked her. Nothing as hot and wicked and naughty and erotic.

Jason's blue eyes darkened as Penelope hurriedly grabbed what looked like a bottle of lube from her nightstand, then crawled onto the bed on all fours, giving him an ample view of her backside. "You can take me in the same way," she urged, smacking her own ass with a loud slap in order to tempt him. "Wouldn't you like that? Wouldn't you like to know how I feel when you stick it inside my ass?"

"Would this please you?" Jason asked softly, a thousand feelings glowing in his eyes.

"Yes, Jason...it really would," she said in a whisper that trembled with desire.

* * * * *

Several memorable times, Jason had had a woman's finger up in his ass, and he'd gloried at the feel of it. Now he felt his asshole clench, the thought of Murry's cock in there making every part of his body suddenly contract, maybe in thrill, maybe in dread.

Murry bit back a smile when Jason nodded ever so slightly. Gathering saliva, Murry spit on his own cock while Jason watched, his eyes heavy and dark as Murry slowly spread the saliva all over his cock with his hand.

Jason walked determinedly toward the bed, heading toward his prize, toward the delectable Penelope on all fours, her little pink ass puckered and ready for him. His eyes feasted on her body as he rested one knee on the edge of the bed, positioning his cock right between the soft swell of her buttocks.

Murry followed him, cupping Jason's waist with two big, calloused hands as Jason took the lube from Penelope's hand and slowly spread it over himself. He handed the bottle to Murry, who added the slick substance to his already shining, saliva-lubed cock.

His cock pulsing, the plum-shaped head engorged and damp, Jason slowly, very slowly, guided his dick into Penelope's ass. She yelped in pain, shuddered with pleasure, and Jason gripped her waist, withdrew and moved inside her again, harder this time.

With the gentleness of experience, Murry held Jason in place and lightly probed his ass with the tip of his cock, using it to slowly part and widen his entrance. Dragging air into his lungs, Murry moved forward another inch, the effort to hold back making his thick muscles tremble.

Jason gritted his teeth as he felt his ass open, widen, stretch. Then in one slow stroke, Murry pushed his dick, big and thick and large, all the way inside him. Jason cried out a harsh, pained sound, and still he felt the pleasure in that pain. Sweating profusely now, Jason began a slow, carnal rhythm as he sank deep into Penelope's burning tunnel, watching in fascination as his cock entered the back of her body. The same way Murry's cock entered his.

Every time Jason withdrew, Murry entered him with a single furious thrust, and every time Jason entered Penelope, Murry withdrew from him. It was killing him, so much pleasure and so unexpected…

Penelope was burning hot, seemingly desperate for release. She yelped and begged and touched herself, cupping her pussy and wildly stroking the nub of her clit.

Murry pressed his chest against Jason's back and licked his ear while he brushed his hands caressingly over his hips.

Groaning, Jason cocked his head sideways and kissed him, thrusting his tongue past his lips and tasting Murry's hot male mouth in desperation. His body shivered at the power in Murry's hands, the warm, seductive strokes of his tongue and the sure, pounding thrusts of his cock.

Murry lowered his hand so he could touch the base of Jason's cock each time it slid out of Penelope's ass.

"I like your cock," Murry murmured against Jason's ear. "Do you like mine?"

"Yes," Jason bit out through clenched teeth, ramming more fiercely into Penelope now. She was wild and pliant beneath him, her body a tight, warm heaven compared to the searing, overwhelming invasion of Murry.

As if he knew just where to touch him, Murry moved his hand from Jason's cock and guided it down to his balls, squeezing them gently at the same time he thrust up deep, so deep into Jason's ass that Jason hissed in pain, thinking he would explode. Murry kissed his ear, his hot tongue dipping and licking. Jason's cock throbbed with pressure even as Penelope's tightness clamped around him, the nearby contractions of her pussy rippling his cock, milking him at the same time his ass locked around Murry's thick, swollen cock.

"Tight little asshole," Murry whispered in a low, gravelly voice against his ear. "Like a virgin boy."

Jason groaned, faintly aware of Penelope looking past her shoulder to watch him, to watch Murry fuck him, hard and fast. Could she tell how much he liked it? Could she decipher the look on his face, tightened with hot, straining pleasure? His eyes met hers and he could see the lust there, the pleasure she felt in watching Jason's body spread and pillaged and forced open just as hers was.

She was stroking her pussy as she watched, stroking herself to orgasm and crying out his name. Jason. Her body jerked under his, dragging him with her to a shuddering climax at the same time Murry cried out. They came together, all three of them, in a wild explosion of fire, as if the earth had cracked open and the flames of hell had burst out, scorching them.

For a few long, interminable minutes they were silent, and only after Murry withdrew and began dressing did Jason actually resume breathing.

A wide smile spread Murry's lips as he paused to eye Jason's profile. "Usually I'd charge double for that," he told him. "But in your case, it's on the house."

Jason gritted his teeth, his eyes deadly on the amused escort. "Gee, thanks, you're so *sweet*."

Penelope laughed as she watched the two men. "Murry, thank you so much, it's been so wonderful to meet you. You're a real bargain for two thousand!"

Murry kissed the back of her hand with flair, as if he were a knight of the realm, not some man who was paid to fuck people. Jason felt somewhat annoyed as he watched him leave—but he figured he could be forgiven for being just a tiny bit pissed. He'd just been fucked by a man, for Christ's sake, and all courtesy of... Scowling, he scanned the room for the culprit. Found it lying on its back on the nightstand, almost smirking at him.

The damned spin devil.

Hesitantly, Penelope approached him. Jason narrowed his eyes at her. "I should kill you for this," he said gruffly before shaking his head. "But I can't. I won't." He eyed the spin devil again. "Maybe it's not even your doing at all." It was that damned spin devil, turning him into a *loco*.

Penelope wrapped her arms around his waist and pressed her cheek to his chest. "Oh Jason...tell me, was it fun, was it good?"

He couldn't lie, not to her. "Yeah, it was good."

"But how good? Really *really* good? Did it feel as good as it looked?"

Oh, what the hell, just come out and say it, he thought, silently willing himself to admit it. "Yeah."

She sighed dreamily. "Maybe next time I can use that big fat dildo to play with *you*," she offered with a bat of her eyelashes.

If he hadn't already come three times in one night, Jason was sure he'd have gotten hard *again* at that wicked proposal. Groaning, he bent down and kissed her with all the tumultuous feelings he'd always harbored for her...and all the worry. "What in the world am I going to do with you?"

"Have lots and lots of sex, in every possible way imaginable."

He cocked an eyebrow. "What if I want more?"

"Then take more. Take everything, Jason."

He considered it for a moment. "You scare the shit out of me," he breathed against her face, kissing her once again, greedily, hungrily. "I don't want to hurt you. Disappoint you. What if I can't give you want you want?"

She stroked his arms, beaming up at him. "You won't disappoint me, and I won't ask for anything but what you can handle giving."

A look of concern crossed his face. "I'm not sure I can handle *you*. You're a real handful—you always have been," he said worriedly, brushing a damp string of hair away from her face. She moaned a little, luxuriating in the feel of his hand on her face, his warm, big body pressed to her softer one, his chest crushing her nipples.

"If you keep me really occupied I'm sure I won't have time to get into any trouble," she promised.

"So should I just tie you to the bed and pleasure you every second of every day and every night? Will that keep you adequately busy?"

"Hmm, definitely."

He bent and took one nipple into his mouth, lightly suckling it before dragging his lips up her throat, her jaw, pausing on her earlobe as a thought struck him. "What do we do with your toy?"

She stared at him, clearly surprised by his question. "Play with it, of course. Spin it more and more and then some more. That's the best toy ever! Best *sex* ever," she added with enthusiasm.

Jason jerked backward, horrified. "If I can even *live* through it, you mean."

She laughed, rumpled Jason's tousled blond hair and blew a cutesy kiss at the object on the nightstand. "He'll make sure you do, won't you, you little cutie? Besides, he'll make all my naughtiest dreams come true—and *yours* too."

"He already did, I'm afraid. The term 'careful what you wish for' certainly applies." At her stricken expression, he laughed, a low rumbling sound, and then cupped her face. "You're more than I bargained for, baby."

All the love in the world shone in her eyes as she smiled up at him. "Then maybe we should bargain with it again, see what you get this time."

He encircled her with his arms, pressing her against him with a smile. "Maybe we should kick its little red ass out of here."

She smacked him playfully on the shoulder. "Don't be so mean to it, Jason. Now—whoever gets the pitchfork toward them gets to take orders. Deal?"

He groaned, knowing with his luck, *he'd* be the one taking orders.

"Deal, Jason?" she prodded, puppy-eyed and beautiful.

Aw, hell and damnation. "Yeah, deal," he agreed.

Giggling, she linked her fingers through his and dragged him across the room toward the spin devil.

"What the hell are you doing, Penelope?" he asked, exhausted and knowing he might not like the answer.

"What does it look like? I'm going to spin some more!"

The End

Also by Red Garnier

ഉ

eBooks:

Amatista

Bona Fide Liar

Devilish Games 1: Spin Devil

Devilish Games 2: Spin It Again

Devilish Games 3: Spin Some More

Divine Assistant

Seven Sinners

Print Books:

Amethyst Attraction *(anthology)*

About the Author

ഔ

Red Garnier is a multi-published erotic romance author. She's also a happy wife and proud mother of two little handfuls. Writing has been her passion since she read her first romance novel at the age of fourteen. Red loves a good laugh, a good cry, but most of all, she loves a good romance. She's thrilled to be able to share her very own stories with others, and hopes you will enjoy reading them as much as she does writing them.

Red Garnier welcomes comments from readers. You can find her website and email address on her author bio page at www.ellorascave.com.

Tell Us What You Think

We appreciate hearing reader opinions about our books. You can email us at Comments@EllorasCave.com.

Why an electronic book?

We live in the Information Age—an exciting time in the history of human civilization, in which technology rules supreme and continues to progress in leaps and bounds every minute of every day. For a multitude of reasons, more and more avid literary fans are opting to purchase e-books instead of paper books. The question from those not yet initiated into the world of electronic reading is simply: *Why?*

1. ***Price.*** An electronic title at Ellora's Cave Publishing and Cerridwen Press runs anywhere from 40% to 75% less than the cover price of the exact same title in paperback format. Why? Basic mathematics and cost. It is less expensive to publish an e-book (no paper and printing, no warehousing and shipping) than it is to publish a paperback, so the savings are passed along to the consumer.

2. ***Space.*** Running out of room in your house for your books? That is one worry you will never have with electronic books. For a low one-time cost, you can purchase a handheld device specifically designed for e-reading. Many e-readers have large, convenient screens for viewing. Better yet, hundreds of titles can be stored within your new library—on a single microchip. There a variety of e-readers from different manufacturers. You can also read e-books on your PC or laptop computer. (Please note that Ellora's Cave does not endorse any specific brands.

You can check our websites at www.ellorascave.com or www.cerridwenpress.com for information we make available to new consumers.)

3. *Mobility.* Because your new e-library consists of only a microchip within a small, easily transportable e-reader, your entire cache of books can be taken with you wherever you go.

4. *Personal Viewing Preferences.* Are the words you are currently reading too small? Too large? Too... ANNOYING? Paperback books cannot be modified according to personal preferences, but e-books can.

5. *Instant Gratification.* Is it the middle of the night and all the bookstores near you are closed? Are you tired of waiting days, sometimes weeks, for bookstores to ship the novels you bought? Ellora's Cave Publishing sells instantaneous downloads twenty-four hours a day, seven days a week, every day of the year. Our webstore is never closed. Our e-book delivery system is 100% automated, meaning your order is filled as soon as you pay for it.

Those are a few of the top reasons why electronic books are replacing paperbacks for many avid readers.

As always, Ellora's Cave and Cerridwen Press welcome your questions and comments. We invite you to email us at Comments@ellorascave.com or write to us directly at Ellora's Cave Publishing Inc., 1056 Home Avenue, Akron, OH 44310-3502.

ELLORA'S CAVE
Romanticon

Annual convention
for women who
refuse to behave

Discover for yourself why readers can't get enough
of the multiple award-winning publisher

Ellora's Cave.

Whether you prefer e-books or paperbacks,

be sure to visit EC on the web at
www.ellorascave.com

for an erotic reading experience that will leave you
breathless.

Made in the USA
Lexington, KY
09 June 2014